Read
B.G. Thomas

Winter Heart

"*Winter Heart* by B.G. Thomas was a powerful story of hope and recovery with a beautiful happy ever after that was hard fought, but so well deserved."

—Joyfully Jay

"The treasure in this story is Wyatt. I got an unfiltered look into his heart and what I saw is unforgettably beautiful."

—Alpha Book Club

Autumn Changes

"There are so many wonderful elements, from the well-crafted plot to the range of emotions."

—Inked Rainbow Reads

Red

"I think it is one of those books that will allow me to discover something new every time I read it. Truly amazing!"

—Rainbow Book Reviews

"I urge you all to give this hot, sweet and poignant story a read."

—The Novel Approach

By B.G. Thomas

All Alone in a Sea of Romance
All Snug
Anything Could Happen
The Beary Best Holiday
Party Ever
Bianca's Plan
The Boy Who Came
In From the Cold
Christmas Cole
Christmas Wish
Derek
Do You Trust Me?
Desert Crossing
Grumble Monkey and the Department Store Elf
Hound Dog and Bean
How Could Love Be Wrong?
It Had to Be You
Just Guys
With Noah Willoughby: Mele Kilikimaka
A More Perfect Union
(Multiple Author Anthology)
Red
A Secret Valentine
Soul of the Mummy
Editor: A Taste of Honey (Dreamspinner Anthology)
Until I Found You

GOTHIKA
Bones (Multiple Author Anthology)
Spirit (Multiple Author Anthology)
Contact (Multiple Author Anthology)

SEASONS OF LOVE
Spring Affair
Summer Lover
Autumn Changes
Winter Heart

Published by DREAMSPINNER PRESS
www.dreamspinnerpress.com

DO YOU TRUST ME?

B.G. THOMAS

Published by
DREAMSPINNER PRESS

5032 Capital Circle SW, Suite 2, PMB# 279, Tallahassee, FL 32305-7886 USA
www.dreamspinnerpress.com

Do You Trust Me?
© 2017 B.G. Thomas.
Lyrics from "Right Outta Nowhere" and "Falling in Love with the Wind" by Christine Kane.
Copyright © 2004 by Firepink Music. All rights reserved. Used by permission of the artist.

Cover Art
© 2017 Anne Cain.
annecain.art@gmail.com
Cover content is for illustrative purposes only and any person depicted on the cover is a model.

ISBN: 978-1-63533-273-5
Digital ISBN: 978-1-63533-274-2
Library of Congress Control Number: 2016915095
Published February 2017
v. 2.0
First Edition published as Trust Me by Amber Quill Press, 2011.

Printed in the United States of America

This paper meets the requirements of
ANSI/NISO Z39.48-1992 (Permanence of Paper).

This one is for Chris Miles and Sally Davis,
the queens of betaing, and selfless friends
I've never had the pleasure of meeting face-to-face
It will happen!

For Trace Zaber, for believing in this story the first time.

And for Angelia Sparrow, the friend and writer who pointed the way.

Acknowledgments

SPECIAL THANKS to...

Julie and Mike Williams for an amazingly "mystic-al" afternoon and teaching me to ride!

All the people who brought this book into a new light. The original edition of this story, as much as I appreciated it, was not what I had dreamed. It ended way too early and left out too much. Now you are reading what I always wanted this book to be.

Elizabeth North and Lynn West for believing in this story and giving it a second chance.

Matthew Ryan and Cristina Manole for proofreading extraordinaire.

And Noah Willoughby for more help than can be imagined.

When courage finally comes
You never see it coming
—Christine Kane

CHAPTER 1
An Unexpected Request

"YOU WANT me to go to a *dude* ranch?" I asked, my eyes agoggle in surprise.

"In Owen's place," Amy replied. Her voice was quiet but strong and did not waver.

Owen. I sighed. Her husband. Her deceased husband.

"Owen was so determined he'd make it. At least this far. He wanted it so much." She paused. "The kids need this, and frankly... well, so do I."

"But a dude ranch?" While my late wife Emily's sister didn't know me as well as Emily had, Amy and I had still been friends for years, especially the last two. She *knew* I was not the outdoorsy type. And horses terrified me. They had ever since one had thrown me at a church camp when I was a kid. Sometimes I had dreams of one of the beasts, the size of the Trojan horse, snorting and rolling its eyes wildly, and I'd wake up in a cold sweat.

I shuddered.

"The trip's all paid for. It would be stupid for me to cancel. And after this, I don't know if we'll ever go back. The kids are growing up. I certainly won't want to go all by myself. This was more for them anyway."

I nodded. The whole family loved that ranch. Big Bear Ranch or Wild Bear... something like that. They'd even taken my daughter with them—for years.

"I think," she said with a sigh, "it'll be a good way to say good-bye to Owen. Our favorite place...." Then she looked up at me and her eyes were glassy. Tears? Amy? But instead of crying, she gave a little laugh. "Kids? Did I say 'the kids'?" She laughed again. "We went for Owen. God, he loves... loved... that place. He fashioned himself a real cowboy."

She wiped at her eyes with the back of her hand, and to my surprise I found I was laughing a little. Owen, a cowboy? It sure explained why he wore that damned cowboy hat every single year when they got home.

At least for a week or so. Then reason would assert itself, and the hat would disappear somewhere in the house.

"Yes," she said with a half smile. "A good way to say good-bye. Show him honor, you know? One more time?"

I nodded once, trying to understand.

"Which is why I wanted to know if you'd please come. It'll be easier, you know? You might help fill the void that's going to be there. And Owen's left a mighty big void. It'll be a lot less lonely for me, you know…?"

"But a dude ranch?" I asked again. Outside? Heat? Bugs? And… horses?

Amy looked at me in that I-can-read-your-mind way of hers (and sometimes I wondered if she could). "Neil, you're not going to be sleeping on the ground or having to rub two sticks together to start a fire. It's not like church camp. The cabins are nice. Very modern. They have their own bathrooms and everything. Showers even. No communal showers, okay? And you don't have to do *anything* you don't want to do. You don't have to ride one single horse—not even one time. Just…." Her voice caught. "Keep me company?"

"Okay," I agreed suddenly, holding up my hand. "I'll go."

I made the decision just like that before I could change my mind. It was the look on her face that did it. The slump of her shoulders and the tone in her voice. All of this was so *not* Amy. Not the always strong woman I'd known for half my life. She'd borne so much with Owen's death. Now a vacation seemed to be tearing her down. And I couldn't stand that. Couldn't stand to see her that way. She really was the strongest person I'd ever known. Stronger even than Em.

Amy had, for all intents and purposes, saved me when my wife died. She had been there for me. Every day. Getting me through it. Could I be there any less for her now that she had lost her husband?

"I'll go," I said again as she looked at me with those blue-green eyes of hers. Usually I could only see the green when the lights were right or the sun was shining on her face. Her near tears had brought out the blue.

"You mean it, Neil?" she asked. She bit her lip, and I knew she was fighting back tears. She was an Olsen after all, and Olsen women did not show weakness.

"I mean it," I said, turning the words "nice cabins with showers" into a mantra in my mind.

Amy surprised me by stepping right up to me, laying her head on my chest, and wrapping her arms around my waist. I'm a big man, at least compared to her. Amy was even more petite than Emily had been, and when I put my arms around her, she practically disappeared. It was like holding my daughter, Crystal. She even had the same fall of wavy auburn hair as Em and Crystal. Like almost everyone in the Olsen family.

Cancer had taken months to kill her husband, and I couldn't figure out which of the two of us had the better deal. The aneurysm had taken Em in a heartbeat; I'd had no time to prepare. No time to say good-bye. Owen, on the other hand, had lived for nearly a year. Nine months, a little longer. Ten. I wasn't sure. Amy had been given the chance to try to prepare herself—if anyone can prepare themselves for losing the love of their life. But the horror of Owen's lingering disease made me wonder if it had been a good thing in the long run. To watch Em waste away would have driven me insane.

"It's all right," I told her and hugged her tight.

She was taking her family on their traditional annual family vacation—without her husband, without her children's father. Me? I couldn't imagine why she would want to go to her family's favorite place in the world. I wouldn't—or couldn't—in the same circumstance. Owen had only been dead for two months. Em had been gone for almost exactly two years, and I still wasn't living. Not really.

I'd wanted to sell the house, get rid of *everything* in it—anything that would remind me of Emily. I couldn't sleep in our room for months. I'd slept on the couch instead. How could Amy go back, with her kids, to the ranch they had gone to every summer for years? Wouldn't every cabin, every building, every horse, every bend in the river, every chorus of "Home on the Range" around the campfire remind her of Owen?

Wouldn't his ghost be everywhere?

But different people cope with grief in different ways, and she was, after all, an Olsen. The whole family was strong, the women especially. So where I'd wanted to flee from anything that reminded me of my wife, Amy wanted to bathe in all things that reminded her of Owen. She thought that was a good way to say good-bye. Who was I to say which was better?

Because really, if Amy hadn't shown up a few weeks after Em's death and kicked me in the ass, I might still be sleeping on the couch.

I probably wouldn't even have a job. She had to remind me I had responsibilities, to my daughter if nothing else.

Thank goodness for Amy. At a time when she should've been grieving herself—Em had been her sister twice as long as she had been my wife, after all—she helped me deal with my own pain.

So yes, even though a week at a dude ranch sounded like the last way on Earth I would want to spend my vacation time, it was something I would do.

I didn't really have a choice.

AFTER DINNER—PIZZA Hut delivery, half-and-half: pepperoni for me, Hawaiian-style for Crystal—I googled Black Bear Dude Ranch. Crystal, who was trying (not too successfully) to do her homework, was thrilled, bubbling over even, ever since she'd heard I was going. She'd been sure her Black Bear days were behind her. Crystal had gone with Amy and her family since she was about ten. Owen had always insisted on taking her. He wouldn't even let me and Em pay her way. They could certainly afford it. Owen had been a lawyer for a major firm, and Amy, comfortable in her own right with family money, was a very successful Realtor. That was saying something with the market the way it'd been over the last decade or so. And she rarely represented a home that cost less than a million dollars.

Funny that I'd never checked up on my daughter's annual vacation spot in all the years she'd been going. Em had always handled stuff like that, and I'd let her. Sure, I'd glanced at the brochures, but that was it. I'd nodded at the photographs afterward and agreed that yes, yes, that was a pretty horse, Crystal (even though I couldn't comprehend her enthusiasm). I listened to her tales of camping (on the ground—God!) and swimming in the river and wrangling cattle (whatever that meant). She loved those vacations with all her heart, and I had only been able to pretend any interest of my own.

Had that made me a crappy husband and father? It was one more thing that Amy had reminded me of. My duty to Crystal. How could I wallow in my grief when there was my daughter to take care of? I could only hope I'd stepped up to the plate since then. I thought I had. Crystal had said little things that made me think so.

The dude ranch's website surprised me. Its official name was Black Bear Guest Ranch, which seemed much less... I don't know... dude-y? I mean, what the hell is a "dude" ranch anyway? A place where dudes hang out?

Black Bear Guest Ranch was not the nightmare I'd imagined. Yes, there were lots of pictures of people riding horses—of course. But the ranch didn't look as rustic as I had feared. I wasn't all that excited to see some of them herding cattle. Herding cattle! I couldn't imagine wanting to do anything like that. The website explained that Black Bear, like so many others, was a "working ranch." Why would anyone want to use their vacation "working" when they could relax by a pool or enjoy cocktails without guilt?

Because—the site further explained glowingly—it gave vacationers a feel of what it was like to live in the Old West.

Yeehaw!

Not my thing.

The good news was the pictures really did make Black Bear Guest Ranch look beautiful. The landscape was lovely—I couldn't deny it— with rolling hills, trees, streams, and a lake (if a sixteen-acre body of water qualified). There was even a real pool, cement and built-in, thank God. The idea of swimming in a dirty river or lake with... with fish and snapping turtles and God knows what else was a lot less appealing to me than to my daughter. But more, there was a dry sauna, Jacuzzi-slash-hot tub, weight room, and a spa. Massages were available, and I imagined after a day in the saddle I'd need one.

And yes, Amy was right. The cabins were lovely. I'd imagined, just as she'd said, something from those enforced church-camp days from my childhood. Large rooms with rows of bunks stacked three high, which were hot in the summer and chilly on wet days, with cold breezes sneaking in from many a crack in the walls and around windows.

In comparison to that grisly image, the rooms at Black Bear appeared rustic only in design. On the outside, they did look a lot like log cabins, only extended, with multiple doors. Pictures revealed that was because there were private rooms, several per building, like a motel. Surprisingly, though, they were more like time-share condos than motel rooms, but a rich, modern cowboy version instead of one from the Old West. The walls were bright pine with prints hanging on them, the rooms nicely furnished, including large, comfortable-looking beds. The bathrooms were completely modern, with large tubs and showers. And some had bearskin rugs.

And the food! The breakfasts looked fit for an army of guests. Dinner included steak, barbecue, grilled salmon and fresh-caught rainbow trout, Cornish game hens, and even buffalo. Plates were heaped high and obviously not designed for vegetarians or those on a diet. I was going to gain a ton! You'd *have* to work on your vacation unless you wanted to come home two pants sizes bigger. Looking at all that food made my mouth water, and I had just eaten.

Of course, Pizza Hut hardly compared to the feasts pictured.

This might be fun after all, I thought.

Emphasis on "might."

And wouldn't it be nice to get away? Go someplace completely different?

As I was about to sign off, my eye caught on a button reading Things You Should Bring. Now that was something I needed to look at. I didn't want to get there only to find out I was missing something important, re the time Em and I had gone to Orlando only to realize I'd forgotten swim trunks and we had no sunblock for her. Which was pretty silly considering swimming was what one generally did when going to Orlando—certainly at a resort. And Em, like all the Olsens, was not only redheaded, but pale. She burned easily. So yeah, I didn't want to show up at the ranch looking for all the world like the rube I was.

Only, in my haste, I missed the button with my mouse and hit Our Staff instead.

A large picture of some two dozen people appeared on my screen. A lot of them looked young, twenties at the oldest, and all smiled at the camera. And, of course, all wore cowboy hats. They seemed to radiate good cheer, each beaming face saying, *Yup, this is where you want to spend your vacation*. Black Bear Guest Ranch. Where else?

Ah, those faces. To be that young again. Was it a requirement to be attractive to work there?

One young man leapt out at me. Well built, his smile sweet—this was no fake smile, because it could be seen in his eyes as well. And his eyes were so unique. I couldn't tell what color they were, but they looked a tad Asian. Or maybe he was one of those people who squinted their eyes when they smiled? Whatever the reason, he was dazzling.

A few more clicks of my mouse and I found a picture of him alone on horseback, and I could see he was quite muscular. He was a wrangler, the site indicated, although it didn't give his name. Apparently Black Bear Guest Ranch usually took on about thirty guests at a time, and a wrangler was assigned to no more than four or five people. In the case of a large family, two wranglers were assigned to them.

Damn. He looked like my daughter's type. I'd have to watch Crystal around him.

In that almost-psychic way of hers, Crystal was suddenly standing behind me and leaning over my shoulder. "Oh," she exclaimed. "That's Cole! I just adore him."

"You do?" My inner father alarms started going off. "How come I haven't heard about this 'Cole'? How old is he?"

"Oh God, Pops. He's old. Twenty-five at least."

I almost laughed. What did she think of me? I must be ancient.

"Besides, Cole's gay," she said matter-of-factly.

I froze. Gay? I looked back at the screen. He was gay? "He doesn't look gay," I whispered.

"Oh, Pop, *please*. What d'you think? Gay guys wear dresses or something?" She put a hand over her mouth and giggled. "Well, *some* do. Drag queens."

"What do you know about drag queens?" I asked—snapped out—in surprise. Damn. Where had she come up with this stuff? Drag queens? Gay wranglers? "They let a gay man work at a family ranch?"

Crystal rolled her eyes in the way only eighteen-year-olds can. "Pop, it's the twenty-first century, for goodness sake. Gays are here to stay. Sorry if you don't like it. They can get married now too, you know."

For a moment, I didn't say anything. I was stunned. It was the last attitude I'd expected my daughter to have. Had times changed that much since I was her age? "And you're okay with that?" I managed.

Crystal nodded. "Oh yeah," she said with delight, giggling and waggling her eyebrows. "Two boys kissin' is hot!"

I reeled back in shock. My stomach had clenched so tight it was hurting. "Kissing? You've seen this 'boy' kissing other boys?"

"God no, Dad."

"Then what...?"

She pointed at the computer. "You've heard of the Internet."

"So?"

Once more she rolled her eyes.

It hit me then. She'd been looking up all kinds of stuff I'd never imagined on the Internet. I was a shitty father. It had never occurred to me to monitor what she did on the computer.

"Don't worry, Dad. I haven't been going to porn sites." Crystal sighed dramatically, then reached out and touched my shoulder. "Pop, it's the way it is. Some people are gay. They can't help it." She gave me a sympathetic smile and turned and left the room.

They can't help it?

Well, she may think—as the typical teenager did—that she knew everything. But about that, she was wrong. They could help it.

Who knew that better than I did?

CHAPTER 2
Getting There

THE DRIVE from Terra's Gate via Kansas City down to Arkansas was fairly uneventful, but beautiful. The farther we drove—it was about six hours in all—the lovelier the countryside became. It was an amazing day, not too cool and not too hot. Roll-down-your-windows weather versus blast your air conditioner. Perfect.

The sky was a color that usually only appeared in paintings—a dazzling, cloudless, robin's-egg blue. Even the air was sweet. There was no smell of chemicals or exhaust or gasoline, only the scent of growing things—clear, clean, and full of promise.

Promise? I wondered. Now where had that analogy come from?

I sat up front with Amy, who was driving, and Crystal was in back with Amy's children—fifteen-year-old Todd, and Robin, who was the same age as my daughter. Like Crystal and so many of Em's side of the family, Robin had red hair. Given my height, build, and dark eyes and hair, my daughter looked more like one of Amy's brood than someone related to me. Only Todd looked anything like me, and we weren't even related by blood.

The two girls chattered like birds (Crystal would be furious with me for saying that), and Todd's nose was buried in some kind of game, like just about any boy his age.

The two weeks since Amy asked me to go on the trip had gone rather smoothly.

I had dreaded going in to work and asking for the time off. After all, I hadn't had the new position that long. But Gary, the manager of Horrell & Howes, surprised me with how quickly he agreed. He seemed happy, almost relieved.

"Yes, you can go. You bet you can go!"

He was a big man, although not the way I was. He wasn't so much tall as... well, round. He reminded me a lot of George from *Seinfeld*—bald, same glasses—but older... plumper.

"Gary! Are you sure? I mean, we're gearing up to one of the busiest parts of our year."

"I'm sure," he said, leaning forward over his desk.

"But…."

He shook his head. "No buts."

"But why?"

He looked at me for a long moment and then asked me to close the door.

Nervous, I got up and did as he asked.

"Neil, I've been worried about you for a very long time. You've been with us for almost three years now, and in the first year, you did nothing but blow me away. Blow a lot of us away. I knew you were meant for more than answering phone calls, even though you were better at it than just about anyone I've seen in all my years here."

He took a deep breath.

"And then…."

I looked away. *Don't say it*, I begged him. Problem was, I didn't say it out loud.

"I only met Emily once. At our Christmas party. She was amazing. She lit up the entire room, you know?"

I knew. She always did that. That's who she was. I had fallen under her spell a long time ago, and she had been the compass in my life, pointing me always true north.

For a long time, Gary didn't say anything. Then finally he did. "I hurt for you, Neil. I really do. When she…."

Don't say it, I thought again. *Don't say "died," and don't say any of those fucking stupid words people use. Those euphemisms for death. Passed. Crossed over. Departed. That I had lost her.*

"You're not living anymore, Neil."

It took everything in me not to lash out at him. But one look from those eyes and I saw the empathy. He wasn't feeling sorry for me. There was no pity. What I saw was not what I was expecting.

It was pure compassion.

"Forgive me for being an asshole," he said then, once more surprising me. Although dammit, Gary was a good man. He had come to Emily's funeral. What boss did that?

"You haven't taken time off in a long time, my friend," he said, and somehow his calling me friend felt good instead of fake. "I want you to go. Take as much time as you want. We owe you four weeks. Take it all if you want."

I sighed.

I saw that he meant it.

I shook my head. "A week is enough," I told him.

He nodded, and I left that office feeling weirdly... what? Why, almost elated.

I'd thought with summer being a busy time for us, there might be a problem, especially because it hadn't been a year since my promotion. Instead, I had been given the golden key and practically a company car.

Oh! That promotion....

IT WAS almost funny how that happened.

Yes, my work had gone to shit after Em died, even after Amy pulled me up by my bootstraps. For months, I hadn't been able to concentrate. Hadn't been able to help the customers like I should have. I was making mistakes—none that Roxanne, the department supervisor, had to be on my back about (at least not much)—but way too many as far as I was concerned. I'd begun to worry I would get fired. At one point, I was a shoo-in for employee of the month almost every month. Taking calls and working with frustrated, hysterical, even weeping people was something for which I had a knack.

But with Em gone, my heart had gone as well. I had to fight-fight-fight the urge to tell angry, even distressed, customers to fuck off. To say, "You think you've got problems? I lost my wife of twenty years. I can hardly get up in the mornings. I cry every time I see our wedding picture hanging in the hall, but I can't bring myself to take it down."

Two years. Two years she had been gone. And I had gone with her. I wasn't living. I had become a good actor. I could smile and nod and make happy. I had even fooled Crystal. Or at least I thought I had. It was hard to tell with a teenager. They were so preoccupied with their own lives and their raging hormones and their belief that they were right and their parents—who had lived at least twice the number of years they had with twice the experience—were wrong.

Not that Crystal was a problem. She didn't disobey me and had only gotten herself into trouble a couple of times, though not in over a year. Nothing serious. It seemed that she had done what I couldn't.

Moved on.

Really moved on.

Then Roxanne went on vacation, and to my surprise, Gary asked me to take over her duties while she was gone. I'd done that a bit here and there, a few hours or a day or two, but two weeks?

Shelia, my team lead, wasn't happy about it, and she did nothing to disguise the fact either. Horrell & Howes was her life. She breathed, lived, and crapped the company. Her very identity was wrapped up in H&H. Me? I took pride in my job. Hell, besides Amy, keeping busy helped me survive. I did a good job, or I wouldn't get the awards, which mostly consisted of getting my picture on a bulletin board and a couple of movie tickets or twenty-dollar gift cards for a local restaurant. Not exactly a trip to Vegas. But I certainly didn't consider Horrell & Howes to be my career. To be honest, I'd never considered any job to be more than a job—never my life's work. To be even more honest, I was one of those who were watching the clock by the end of the day.

But I thought, what the hell, and jumped in. In for a penny, in for a pound, as Em used to say.

I was surprised when, by the third day, I found I was getting into it. There was something about getting off the phone with customers I could no longer sympathize with and instead getting lost in Roxanne's many duties that made me feel like I had purpose again. I kept seeing little things that could be done to improve operations. I found I wasn't watching the clock to see when I could go home, but was checking it to make sure I had time to get things done.

My fellow employees were impressed as well. I knew them. Knew their quirks, their interests, their worries. I made allowances, which brightened their attitudes, even though they knew those allowances would only apply for two weeks. To my delight, call volume went up and complaints were down.

On the second Friday, my last, several of my coworkers even asked me to go out for drinks with them after work. And I went! I had a fun time, getting a buzz I hadn't dared in a long time. Everyone told me how great the last two weeks had been and that they'd be happy to work for me anytime. They said they were sorry I'd be on the phones again the next week.

They were sorry!

The biggest surprise that night—no, the second biggest—happened when I realized one of the ladies, Charleen, had been flirting with me all evening.

"She's hitting on you pretty heavy," said this new guy named Sloan.

"Huh?" I'd asked, slack-jawed.

How I'd missed that until we were ready to go, I don't know. In retrospect, she'd been pretty obvious. We were in the parking lot, and she asked me if I would like to come to her place for dinner sometime. I was startled. She was asking me on a date?

Everything in me rebelled at the idea. I had to tell her I wasn't ready. I think she understood.

The biggest eye-opener, though, was when I told Crystal. Her reaction was explosive.

"No," she'd actually yelled. "No way!"

I'd just looked at her, dumbstruck.

"Pop, you just can't. You *can't*. Please. I can't watch you be with another woman besides Mom. I couldn't. I don't want a stepmother. Not *ever*."

She'd made me promise.

And truly it wasn't a hard promise to make. Not really. I couldn't imagine being with another woman either.

No. Not again.

Em had been special. The one. The only one I could be with like that.

So I never went to dinner with Charleen.

The following week at work was hard, and it was no shock when I was called into Roxanne's office. It was with dread that I saw both the manager, Gary, and someone from Human Resources there as well.

It seemed Roxanne had accepted a transfer to New York, the very same place she had been for "vacation." They wanted me to take her job.

I couldn't believe it.

It was like a ray of sunshine breaking through dark and stormy clouds.

I won't go into all the smiles and patting of backs and handshakes or the "We're impressed" comments.

But I will say life began to get a little better. For the first time since I'd been without Em to encourage me, I was doing something. I was doing it on my own. I won't say I was happy, but gravity seemed a tad less heavy, the air a little easier to breathe.

And to tell the truth, I didn't mind beating Shelia for the position one bit. Not only because she had been such a bitch to me for two weeks, but because she was a bitch to everyone. It had pissed me off when I'd overheard her saying that it was "typical" that they promoted a man instead of a woman. I wanted to believe—needed to believe—that I had deserved it. She worked hard, yes. I couldn't deny that. But she really was a mean person—the kind who would have been thrilled to be in charge so she could write people up and look for excuses to fire them instead of encouraging them and helping them be proud of their jobs. Being a call-center rep wasn't easy. It could be a thankless job even without having to deal with the rude and angry customers who often phoned in.

Shelia was one of those "company people," and she forgot that people—her fellow workers—*were* the company. The heart and soul of any company. She would have been a horrible supervisor, and it had nothing to do with her being a woman.

Horrell & Howes was one of those miracle companies. It hadn't forgotten that their employees counted. That had helped me survive the last two years.

I hadn't had the position a full year when I asked Gary for the vacation time to go to Black Bear and he said yes. "Hell yes!"

IF THE countryside we traveled through was any indication, Black Bear Guest Ranch might be just what I needed, and I found the closer we got, the lighter my heart felt.

I was actually getting excited.

When we got off Highway 5, we went another ten miles or so on a pleasant dirt road, and then we were there.

We stopped at the entrance to the ranch, and everyone scrambled excitedly out of the car. Apparently, the first tradition was for everyone to get their picture taken in the arms of one of the two huge carved bears standing on either side of the ranch's gate. Above was the time-honored arched wrought-iron sign with the words Black Bear Guest Ranch. Everyone insisted I take part, and soon I found myself enfolded in the embrace of a rough-hewn bear that towered at least two feet above my head. This elicited applause from all, and Amy declared I was now a part of the Black Bear family.

Before we could leave, another car pulled over and another group of people, cameras in hand, began to assemble themselves around the bears. So this wasn't only my family's standard way of beginning the week's vacation.

We got back in the car for a short jog down a narrow tree-lined road. Then the road opened up, and we were there. The ranch lay spread out before us. There were more buildings than I'd expected, each in the style of a log cabin. We passed two people on horseback, and I marveled at the size of the animals. Not Trojan-horse-sized, no, but seemingly giant all the same. A sign shaped like a bear—what else?—welcomed us, and another told us guest services was right ahead.

Around a slight bend sat a building that was obviously the place. It was big. And like everything else, quite lovely. I was surprised at the number of people gathered either on or near the building's long front porch. There must have been fifty people standing around and at least twice as many pieces of luggage.

The parking lot was packed, but Amy gave us a whimsical little smile and magically pulled into one of what she called the "rock-star parking spots," right up front. Somehow there was always a space for Amy.

We got out of the car, and another of the carved bears, even larger than the others, loomed over us. It was an impressive sight.

"Mr. and Mrs. Radcliff" came a cry, and a young blonde girl ran up to us and then froze. "Oh my God," she said with a gasp.

Amy turned and forced a smile. "Cassie, how are you?" Amy looked at me. "Neil, this is Cassie, one of the wranglers here."

Then, to the blonde, "Cassie, this is Neil Baxter, Crystal's father."

Cassie's eyes were still wide, and I could see she was horrified, but she put on her best front and held out her hand. "It's nice to meet you, Mr. Baxter." She looked like she was probably in her midtwenties. No girl. This was a young lady.

"It's nice to meet you too, Cassie," I answered, pretending not to notice her mistake. I felt pretty sorry for her. I had opened my mouth and inserted my foot more than once in my life. I wanted to make her feel better. "I take it this isn't your first summer here?"

"Oh no." Her smile broadened slightly. "My sixth."

"You must like it here," I said.

"Oh yeah!" She nodded vigorously, her tight curls bobbing around her round little face. "I love it. I'd live here year-round if I could."

"That's a recommendation if I ever heard one," I replied. If everyone was as sweet as this young woman, it was one more plus, I thought. I looked for Amy and saw she was opening the hatchback.

"Let me help," Cassie said and shot to Amy's side, where I could hear her whisper, "I'm so sorry, Mrs. Radcliff. I feel so bad. I forgot. I—I thought...."

"I know what you thought, dear," I heard Amy say. "It's all right." She hugged the girl. "Now help me with these?"

"Of course!" And together they began to pull our luggage out of the back of the car. Before I could move, Todd jumped in. "Mom! I'm the man of the family now. Let me."

"Okay, then." Amy stepped back to let Todd demonstrate his masculinity. Todd had transformed in size and height during the last year, as surely as Owen had seemed to shrivel away. Unlike his mother and sister, he didn't have red hair. That had done nothing to prevent him from looking like Opie Taylor. But our Opie had metamorphosed into a handsome young man, with a mop of dark hair and even the very beginnings of chest hair—at fifteen! It was so ironic, and sad as well, that Todd changing from boy into man should happen in time for Owen to miss most of it.

A moment later, a pudgy young man raced up with a half-full luggage cart. "Hey, Mrs. Radcliff," he said excitedly and started to place the bags on it with no other preamble.

Amazing was all I could think. Sure, Amy and her family had been coming here for years, but it was only *one* week. How many guests must they have in a year? How did they not only remember her among so many people passing through, but even remember her name?

"Leo, isn't it?" Amy asked, smiling, her eyes lighting up.

And of course they remember her, I thought. *Who wouldn't?*

"Yes, um, ma'am," he said, and blushed. "You remember me?"

Of course she did.

"Of course," Amy said and introduced us. "Leo, this is Crystal's father, Neil Baxter. Neil, Leo."

Leo grinned mightily. "Oh. Hey!" He held out his hand, and when I took it, he gave me an even mightier shake. "Awesome. It's great to meet you. Crystal is way awesome!"

Way awesome? Did I have to watch for him too?

Well, not "too," I remembered. Because Cole was gay. My stomach clenched, and I glanced around me. Was he here? Where was Mr. Some-people-are-gay-they-can't-help-it?

"Now where did Robin and Crystal get off to?" Amy asked and looked at the crowd around the porch. I saw where she was looking and glanced that way myself.

Would I recognize him?

And what the hell was I even looking for him for?

I saw both our daughters hugging some girls about their age. I couldn't miss them with their red hair. Their auburn locks blazed in the sunlight.

You'd never know I was a part of the family. As I said, only Todd looked anything like me, and that was only an accident of genetics. I don't know why, but I had a flash of loneliness, even with so much family and so many people around.

"There they are." I pointed, although from the smile on Amy's face I realized she had already seen them. "Did you want to join them?"

"They're with friends," she replied. "I was just curious. It's not like they aren't safe."

I nodded. Safe. As long as they weren't thrown by horses.

"As long as they watch for rattlesnakes."

My eyes popped. I couldn't help it. "Rattlesnakes?"

She nodded casually. "Western diamondbacks. Timbers. Western pygmies." As if she were talking about the local herbs and birds.

I could feel the color drain from my face. Western diamondbacks? Timbers? Western pygmies?

She nodded again and barely spared me a glance. "But I don't think any of them are particularly deadly."

Particularly deadly?

"I mean, you don't want to be bit by one. It's going to hurt. But they have antivenom here, and the wranglers even carry it on them—I think—so you won't die."

I looked around me. At the ground. Then back to the car. Was it too late to leave? I could check myself into a local hotel and come get everybody when it was time to go home.

"Neil?"

I turned back to her, willing my heart to calm down.

She smiled. "I'm pulling your leg."

I blinked at her. "Huh?"

"Kidding."

"Kidding?"

She nodded, and I was flooded with relief.

You bitch, I mouthed, and she burst into laughter.

"Don't do that," I said. "I'm nervous enough."

"I couldn't help it." She laughed again. "But seriously, there are snakes. The great thing about rattlers is that they warn you. I don't remember anyone ever getting bitten."

I swallowed. Hard. It almost hurt.

"It's the cottonmouths you have to watch out for. They don't warn and they don't run. They lie very still and if you step on them—*bam!*—"

I jumped a foot.

"—they get you."

Oh you bitch, you bitch, you bitch.... And was she being serious or messing with me again?

She looked at me again, her expression both serious and sparkling with mirth. "Relax. Just make sure you're wearing your boots. They can't hurt you, then."

And again, this gave me no relief.

I took a deep breath and tried to think of other things. Like the people. A lot more people than I'd expected. "I can't believe all these people. I thought the website said they took no more than thirty guests. How many people work here?"

"Oh, about ten or fifteen, I'd guess. What with the owners and cooks and housekeeping," Amy explained. "Most of these people are guests, but some are leaving. That's Sunday for you. Guests arrive and guests leave. For an hour or two, it's orchestrated chaos. The people who've been here all week will leave, and we'll have lunch while the staff madly cleans the rooms. I bet it's a sight." She laughed. "I need a cleaning person at my house like that!"

Amy had gone through quite a few housecleaners in her time. She had a very high standard for her home, especially after having to make sure it was clean enough during Owen's sickness.

Me? Since Em's death, I'd done the best I could. I couldn't afford to have someone in. Em had always been the real breadwinner, and that wasn't even counting her share of the Olsen money. I'd gone through many a job before settling in at the call center. Because of the economy, one office after another closing down seemed to follow me like a bad dog. It wasn't until my promotion that I even made close to anything Em had ever made. Which had kept me from losing the house and had kept the utilities running. I was lucky Crystal had such good grades and Em's mother had set up a healthy trust fund for her college education. Plus what Emily had left her, of course. Otherwise it would have been community colleges and local universities. Not that Wagner U was anything to scoff at—and local residents got a discount and didn't have to live on campus. Crystal, though, had her sights set on other places. One, in fact, not far from this ranch. Or at least a lot closer to Black Bear than Terra's Gate. She needed to get away from small-town life, even if the town where she'd grown up wasn't all that small—it was a college town, after all—and even though it was only about forty-five minutes from Kansas City with its population of nearly half a million people, two million counting the metro area.

At that moment, an elderly couple stepped out onto the porch.

"Come on," Amy said. She took my hand and led me to the crowd. "That's the Clarks. They own Black Bear."

I went with her up the short walk to the porch. A line of wind chimes filled the air with tinkling music.

"Good morning, everyone," the slightly plump woman said. She had her hair pulled back to accommodate a sky-blue cowboy hat. "To all of you who are leaving today, we hope you had a wonderful stay and that we'll see you next year. Vincent and I loved having you, and our staff did as well. They tell me you're about the best darned group we've ever had."

"She always says that," Amy whispered in my ear.

"For all our new guests, welcome! I'm Darla Clark and this is my husband, Vincent."

Vincent was thinner and slightly taller than his wife. He reminded me of the man in the famous painting of the farm couple where the husband is holding a pitchfork (although Darla looked completely different from that wife). He had a slight smile that looked like it might have been painted on. His eyes, though, were bright and alert. Amused, even.

"We hope this is the best week of your whole year," Darla continued. "It is *so* good to see familiar faces. Mr. and Mrs. Williams, welcome back. Mr. and Mrs. Beeler, we've missed you. Oh, Mrs. Radcliff! So good to see you and your family."

Wow, I thought. This was real. Just like those kids, she remembers people she only sees once a year. Remarkable given the number of people she must see for months on end. It was one thing for the guests to recognize each other. They only had each other to remember. But Darla? How many months was Black Bear open to the public? How many people did she have to remember? And by name!

"For all you first-timers, we hope you find out fast why so many of our guests come back year after year."

Year after year. It wasn't only Amy and her family. Who would imagine taking the same vacation every year?

"Now, while your rooms are being prepared and your luggage handled, why don't you all come in and have lunch?"

There was much excitement, and those of us who weren't leaving headed for the double doors Darla indicated. That took us past the Clarks, of course, and she hugged each of us, while Vincent passed out either hugs or handshakes, depending on some reasoning to which I wasn't privy.

Darla hugged Amy extra tight. "I'm so sorry about Mr. Radcliff," she said, true sincerity in her voice. She looked like she might cry. "We sure are going to miss him around here."

Vincent—obviously the quiet type—simply nodded.

"Thank you so much. We miss him too," Amy said, and they hugged again.

"You must be Crystal's father," Darla said, turning to me and giving me a strong hug.

The warmth of it took the edge off my surprise.

"Yes, I am, ma'am."

"You can't deny her, can you? Woulda known it if you hadn't been standing here with Mrs. Radcliff."

"Really?" I said, and damned if a tear didn't suddenly threaten my eye. I had just been thinking Crystal didn't look anything like me.

"We sure do love that daughter of yours. She's something special. We've practically watched her grow up."

She had, I realized. Crystal had been coming here for... how long? Since she was eight? Seven?

"Thank you." I liked Darla already. She reminded me of my own grandmother.

Vincent leaned in, took my hand, and gave it a strong shake. "She is a great gal," he said. "We're kinda hopin' she'll join the Black Bear family once she graduates."

Huh? I was surprised, but before I could say anything, Amy drew me into the building. We found ourselves in a large dining hall, guarded by a huge stuffed bear that stood just inside.

"Jesus," I said, staring at its paws and the incredibly long and vicious-looking claws.

"Vincent shot it several years ago," Todd said, excited. "Ain't it dope?"

"Isn't it," Amy corrected.

"*Isn't* it," Todd said with great exaggeration.

"They've got bears on their property?" I asked, incredulous.

"Pop," Crystal said, characteristically rolling her eyes, "this is Black *Bear* Guest Ranch!"

"Bears?" I repeated. Bears? Forget Trojan horses. Forget fucking snakes! *Bears?*

"They haven't had one in quite a few years," Amy reassured me and patted my back. "I don't think you need to worry about them."

"Famous last words," I muttered. Bears?

Amy waved me into the dining hall, and even though I'd already seen the photos from the website, I was still pleasantly surprised. It was a large room, paneled in pine except for one stone wall with a giant fireplace. A dozen or so round tables were arranged around the room, seating about six people each. Some were most likely for the staff since there were more than enough seats for the guests.

At the first table, I saw place cards with names on them. "Assigned seating?" I asked.

"For this meal," Amy explained. "So we can get matched up with our wrangler."

As long as it it's not the gay one.

"I sure hope we get Cole again," my daughter said.

"Crystal," I said a little too loudly. "You want *him*?" I glanced around me, hoping no one had heard the distaste in my voice.

"Neil!" Amy hushed me. "What's wrong with Cole?" She looked surprised.

"How about the fact he's homosexual?" I asked seriously.

Amy looked at me like I'd gone out of my mind, which only made it worse.

"You're okay with that?" I asked. "Don't you think it's inappropriate? This is a family place. Do you want our daughters around that?"

"Neil," Amy said, "I can't believe you're saying that. Cole is a very nice young man. And hell, why wouldn't I want him around our daughters? At least I don't have to worry about him being 'inappropriate.' Plus he shows our girls that gay men are just people. It teaches them to appreciate the diversity in this world. I never had any idea you needed the same lesson."

To my surprise, I saw that she was angry at me. I was speechless. I could count on one hand the number of times she'd been mad at me in the over three decades we'd known each other. I looked around the table at eyes just as hostile. Even Todd seemed upset.

Finally, trying to show her how incensed I was, I asked, "How did Owen feel about him?"

At that, Amy shook her head and the tension seemed to run out of her. "Owen? I don't think he even knew. Owen could be so obtuse about certain things. He might have missed it if Cole made love to a man right on this table."

Immediately, the image of two men lying naked in each other's arms filled my mind. On our table. *No!* I thought, trying to push the picture away.

"Hey, everybody" came a loud and happy voice.

"Oh my *God*," Crystal all but shouted. "Are you our wrangler?"

"I sure am, sweetie. You didn't think I was going to let anybody else have you, did you?"

I turned in my chair to see a stunning young man standing over us with a huge platter of food.

It was Cole.

The gay one.

CHAPTER 3
Cole and Mystic

SOME PEOPLE don't look like their pictures. The photographs do something to them. Make them look older or heavier or paler or puffier. Catches them with one eye half-closed or heavy-lidded, so they looked drunk or drugged out. Or with a strange sneer. Or maybe while they're moving so everything is a blur.

I think I'm the most unphotogenic person in the world. Em and I had to spend hours going through wedding pictures before I found one I didn't mind hanging on our wall.

None of this was true about Cole.

He looked *just* like his pictures—and more. If his photos had been good, in person he looked even taller, more muscular, and better-looking. He could've been a model or a movie star instead of a wrangler on a dusty ranch. His rolled-up sleeves revealed muscular arms bulging from the weight of the food he was holding. And those arms, they were so smooth, whereas mine were hairier. *Would his chest be smooth too?* I wondered.

Shit! Why did I care about that?

His smile was even more dazzling (and more disarming). And then there were his eyes.

Oh, those eyes! *Intense.* They were a deep, dark chocolate-brown, and so.... I struggled to find the right word. Exotic. Once again, I wondered if he had some mixed Asian ancestry because of their almost almond shape. His hair, dark brown as well, was cut fairly short, and it suited him perfectly. Made him look even more masculine.

Which is what he was—and more.

I found I wasn't breathing and had to tell myself to inhale.

Cole set the tray down, and when he did, he was standing almost directly over me. I could smell him. He smelled like country, sunshine, and clean, honest man. I was finally breathing, and what I was breathing was the scent of him (even as I was asking myself what the hell I was doing).

"I hope you're all hungry." His voice was deep and delightful.

It was only when my brain connected that I smelled the food: open-faced beef sandwiches with mashed potatoes, all smothered in brown gravy, along with baby carrots. Finally something I could focus my attention on that was *not* the young man standing over me.

Cole passed out the plates and asked us what we wanted to drink. My throat was too dry to answer, and Amy, knowing my preference for iced tea, ordered for me with an amused smile and a raised eyebrow. It was like she could see what was happening to me. I looked away from her, but that only forced my attention on Cole's retreating form, and, damn, his pants were tight.

I tore my eyes away from the sight and stared at my plate. Made myself dig in. One bite and it didn't take much to keep my attention there, at least until Cole returned and took the only empty seat at the table—the one next to me.

"You must be Crystal's daddy, right?" he said, unleashing his smile on me.

To my horror, I realized I was getting hard. Sweat began to trickle down my ribs, and once again I had to remind myself to breathe. I tried to answer, couldn't, and nodded instead.

He held out his hand, and I could only stare at it. It was big, with long, square-tipped fingers.

Amy elbowed me, and I jerked and took his hand. For a moment it felt like it was a thousand degrees. I almost flinched.

But no.

It wasn't hot.

It was no warmer than mine.

But it was so… alive. I felt like I'd never shaken hands before.

"I can see it," Cole said. "She looks like you."

"She does?" I said, voice cracking like a teenage boy's. It was the second time someone had said that within minutes. I cleared my throat and repeated, "She does?"

"Your eyes, for one thing," Cole said, leaving his hand in mine. "She's got your eyes."

Was it normal for a man to hold another man's hand this long? Was it long or was I being weird? Time suddenly seemed messed up.

"B-but her eyes are blue," I managed. And my eyes were brown. Ordinary brown. Nothing like Cole's.

I went to pull my hand away, and he held firm for *just* an instant longer. As he finally let go, he gave me a wink.

My heart skipped a beat. No. Several.

Then it hit me. Was he flirting? Was this gay boy flirting with me? In front of everyone?

Cole turned away and began to chat with the others at the table, catching up, catching them up. So Crystal was going away to college, huh? And Robin too? Had they gone to prom? Yes, but not with a boyfriend. No, he was not seeing anyone. Not in quite a while.

I sat there not saying a word. Amy shot me a look, and I shrugged. I took a long drink of my tea and felt better.

It had all been my imagination. All of it. Cole was not flirting. Of course not. And my reaction to him? It was just because it had been a long time since I had interacted with a gay man. I'd learned to dodge them. I could spot them from miles away, and I stayed clear.

I took a deep breath and a big bite of my food. Delicious. I had to use a fork. There was no picking this sandwich up.

Better.

Eating let me change my focus.

I took another drink.

Better.

AFTER LUNCH, Cole announced we were going to give the staff more time with our rooms and go horseback riding. Something had come up—nothing to worry about; it would be solved in a jiff—and the riding would give them a chance to finish the job right.

Plus it would give us the first choices in horses, he said, as if in some way that was supposed to thrill us.

Except it did seem to thrill my family. Apparently, we'd be a day or two up on everyone else.

Luckily, I was wearing the cowboy boots—although mine were the cheap thrift-store variety—the Black Bear website had insisted we'd need. Something about the heel and the stirrup?

And apparently protection from snake bites!

"I want Andromeda," Crystal cried.

"Dusty," called Robin.

Todd joined in. "I want King."

Cole laughed and said he thought he could arrange that, and did Amy have a preference?

"Galavant?" she said almost shyly.

"Galavant it is," Cole said. Damn, was he charming about it. I could see how he melted Amy's heart. And he was gay!

It felt a little funny knowing my daughter and my extended family had favorite horses. I felt left out, and I didn't know why. Hell, I didn't even want to ride a horse!

"What about you?" Cole asked.

Me? I'd just been thinking I didn't want to ride. But how did I tell this man that?

"He's afraid of horses," Crystal chimed in.

Great, I thought. *Just great!*

"Afraid?" Cole gave me a lopsided smile. "Big daddy like you? *Nah*." He shook his head. "No, you're not."

I felt my face heat up. I wanted to deny my fear, but how could I? Especially when it came time to climb onto one of those huge beasts? Couldn't I just go to my room? I didn't care that it hadn't been made up yet. Hey! Swimming. I could go swimming. But Cole was already leading us out of the building at that point, and I found myself following along.

"A horse threw him off when he was a boy," Amy explained. "Broke his arm and hurt his back."

"Ah, okay." Cole nodded at me knowingly. "I *knew* it. You're not afraid of horses. You're afraid of the horse that threw you. And I am willing to bet he's not here."

"Well," I said, and my throat clicked, "I sure don't want to be thrown again."

"Of course not. I wouldn't either. It sucks. And a broken arm? Of course that would make anyone think twice about getting on a horse again. I almost got my tailbone broken once." He reached up and held his chin between thumb and forefinger—a chin with the barest, finely trimmed goatee; not too much more than stubble. Cole looked at me thoughtfully. "You want a good horse, not a wimpy one. No old-lady horse for you, no way. But not a wild one either."

An old-lady horse sounded good to me, but as I looked at the masculine young man, I suddenly didn't want to seem "wimpy" to Cole. I certainly didn't want to seem less masculine than a gay man.

"Gentle and sweet," Cole continued as we walked. "But ready to go hell-bent when *you're* ready." He smiled, and those dark, exotic eyes took on a twinkle. "Mystic," he said.

We had reached the stables, and the others, save for Amy, had already run ahead. I was impressed when we got inside. There were a lot more stalls than I had imagined. And it was very clean.

"How many horses do you have here?" I asked.

"Altogether we have fifty-nine," Cole replied. "There are two more buildings like this one, plus a couple of much smaller ones."

I whistled. Suddenly, I understood the price tag for a week at Black Bear Ranch. I'd known someone who'd owned a horse, and he'd had to sell the animal. Said a horse was a money pit with its upkeep, food, vet appointments, and more. So how much must it cost to take care of nearly sixty horses? And that wasn't even counting their initial cost.

I stood and watched the kids. It made me smile. They knew what they were doing. They'd quickly found the names of their horses on a huge dry-erase board, and they wrote their names next to their horse's to indicate which animal they'd be riding. Then they picked up their horses' saddles and hauled them down into the depths of the stable. Crystal's Andromeda was only a few stalls down, and I marveled at how fearlessly she opened its gate and went inside.

I couldn't imagine myself doing the same. I turned and locked eyes with Amy.

"I'll help you," she said.

"No, no," Cole replied. "You take care of Galavant. I've got Big Daddy here."

I felt a funny little quiver between my shoulder blades and tried to decide if I liked Cole's apparent nickname for me or if it was pissing me off. Right now, it could go either way.

But hell, the way he was looking at me. My insides were churning. I felt almost naked. What was going on?

Cole turned and led me almost to the end of the first row, then stopped where a dark horse had its head sticking out over the stall's gate. "This is Mystic." Cole reached out and stroked the animal's face.

Something happened then that's hard to explain. When I looked at Mystic, the horse was looking right at me.

Its eyes were a deep chocolate brown (almost as dark as Cole's). The depth of those eyes was more than their color. I saw intelligence there. I don't know what I'd expected. Goldfish eyes? The animal was *truly* looking at me, into my eyes, as if it were assessing me. It tilted its head, and, I swear, it looked deeper. Its gaze seemed to be delving *into* me. I couldn't believe what was happening. I felt hypnotized.

Then it appeared to nod, and I was released. I let out a long breath that I didn't know I'd been holding.

What an incredible experience.

Cole placed a hand on my shoulder and said, "She likes you."

"Sh-she does?" I asked.

I was finally able to view the animal as a whole, and I saw just how beautiful a creature she was. She had a head that was mostly brown—an almost reddish brown—except for a path of white down the center of her face, and a long mane that was mostly white with a little black right at the top. Most of the rest of her was white, except for her brown chest, hindquarters, a few patches, and a few matching spots. When she flicked her tail, I saw it was mostly black as well, with a touch of white.

"Appaloosa?" I asked.

"Spotted Saddlebred," he said. "She's registered as an American Saddlebred. More often than not they're show horses rather than ranch horses, but she came to us needing a home and there was no way we could turn her away. Not such a magnificent horse."

I was enthralled. Mystic was magnificent. This creature was not the terror I had conjured up from my dreams, but something almost… why… sacred. No wonder people fell in love with horses. Referred to them as noble beasts.

"I c-can't ride this animal," I said. "It wouldn't be right."

"Of course you can." Cole squeezed my shoulder. He was so close to me I could feel his breath in my ear, his chest against my back. "It would be *most* right. I truly believe God made horses to be our companions. God *made* them to be ridden. And set *us* to be their caretakers."

"You do?" Hadn't I just been thinking Mystic was sacred? Me? Who didn't believe in God or such mumbo jumbo. But Cole? He believed "God" made horses? And made us to be their caretakers?

"You believe in God?" I asked.

"Yes," Cole answered. "Not my mother's God. Not some old man on high, sitting on a giant marble throne, ready to pass down judgment. That doesn't make any sense to me. I can't even imagine what God is. But I do believe. I don't try and put It in a box."

"It?"

"Yes," Cole said. "'Cause God *isn't* a man. How could that be?"

It was a strange, timeless instant as I stood there between Mystic and Cole, feeling things I couldn't understand and listening to a gay man talk about God. To say I had never expected to be in such a situation doesn't begin to explain it. My mother had always told me homosexuals were evil—

(*"Not my mother's God."*)

—yet here I was in the presence of something that felt sacred, listening to Cole—a gay man—talk about the sacred.

I was feeling… I didn't know what. The moment was charged and yet… peaceful. It was good. I wanted it to last forever. I relaxed into Cole, knowing I shouldn't, but unable—unwilling?—to stop myself. It felt good to let go.

I realized I liked it.

"Are you ready?" Cole asked, and it took me a few seconds to understand what he meant.

"I—I guess," I muttered.

"Mr. Baxter, trust me. Okay?"

I took a deep breath and nodded.

"Mystic *wants* you to ride her. She loves it. She's accepted you—I knew she would—and now she's ready. See how she's starting to sort of prance? Her tail flicking? She's ready. She's ready for *you* to be ready."

"You mean all of this, don't you?" I asked.

"I do."

I took a deep breath. Looked at Mystic. Looked at Cole.

How could I tell him no? I glanced back at Mystic.

How could I tell *her* no?

"Okay."

"I'll get her saddle," Cole told me and was gone.

Immediately, I felt the lack of his presence, but Mystic somehow made everything all right. I reached out and, tentatively, touched her face and marveled at how soft it was. And warm. So alive.

I don't know what I had expected, but this vital "aliveness" beneath my palm wasn't it.

Then Cole was back, and he opened the stall door and led me in beside Mystic, told her all was right in the world, and began to saddle her.

Cole showed me how and told me that next time he wanted me to do it, but not to worry. He'd be right there.

"You ready?" he asked again, and, of course, this time I knew what he meant.

"You can do it, Pops," said Crystal.

I looked up to see her leading a lovely gray horse along the aisle outside the stall. Amy was there as well, with a pure black horse. She was smiling—I could see Em in her smile—and then she nodded.

"Okay," I told Cole, and he took Mystic's reins, leading her out into the bright, warm afternoon.

"NOW, BEFORE you climb on, talk to her. Introduce yourself."

Talk to her? Introduce myself?

But I could see in Cole's eyes that he meant it.

I took a deep breath and turned back to Mystic. And she was looking at me. Totally.

I found I was almost trembling.

"It's okay," Amy said from astride her horse, mere feet away. "You don't need to be afraid."

But I wasn't afraid. I don't know what I was, but afraid wasn't it.

Awe, I thought. I was much closer to awe.

"All right," I said and cleared my throat. I reached out and hesitantly stroked her side. The hair was not quite as soft as on her face, but she was so warm. I ran my hand down her neck and did it again. I loved the feel of her. So different from any other animal I had ever touched. "Hey, Mystic, you sure are a pretty girl. I'm Neil."

Did Mystic nod?

"Good, good," Cole said. "Now remember always to mount from the left. Get your foot up."

Easier said than done. The stirrup was high. Really high. And I'm a tall man. How had the others managed it? To get my foot up into it was awkward. How ridiculous did I look with one foot on the ground and the other so high my ass was sticking out....

Damn!

"There, that's it. Grab the horn and bounce on your right foot and.... Let me get you a mounting block."

"A what?"

"It's like a step stool. Even Olympic riders use them. No shame in it, and it saves the saddle and the horse's withers."

"No," I said quickly. For some reason I didn't want to look like a wimp in front of Cole.

Determined, I gave Cole's instructions a try and was embarrassed to see I wasn't going to make it on my first attempt.

Suddenly Cole's hand was on my butt, quick as could be, and with only a slight push I was up, leg over, and settling into the saddle. I could feel the heat where Cole had been so personal, and my balls drew up tight.

I gasped and didn't know if it was because of the intimate touch or the fact I was now on noble Mystic.

Maybe both?

CHAPTER 4
First Time

COLE PUT the reins in my right hand and explained how they worked: pull back to slow or stop her, left and right to guide, a slight, easy kick with my heels against her sides to urge her on.

At first, the ride was a bit unsettling. It was like being in a rocking boat. *I'll be shaken apart in no time.* How did people ride for hours?

"Scooch up a little bit," Cole said. "Scoot your butt forward."

I wasn't sure if I was doing what he wanted, but I tried.

"Good. That's it."

And almost immediately, I felt more comfortable.

"Her bridle is bitless," Cole said. "That means there's no bit, the metal thing that goes in a horse's mouth. I don't like them and neither do the Clarks. The horse's mouth gets tough, and they stop responding. Since we get a lot of novice riders, we want to make things as pleasant and painless for the horses as possible. Most people tend to haul on the reins in a pinch. So many people who come to dude ranches don't have a clue what they're doing—"

"Like me?" I interjected.

"You're doing fine so far. You're on a very good horse too… one of my favorites. Mystic is good. She is very responsive. Some of our older horses are pretty stubborn. Now I'm going to get my horse. I'll take the reins and tie you to this rail here, and I'll be right back, okay?"

I felt a flash of fear, but Cole was so confident I pushed it down. Amy rode up. "I'll watch him," she said.

"All right," Cole said. "You keep the reins, and I'll be right back."

Cole dashed off, and I watched him go. He was pure grace, like a horse himself. When he entered the stables, I turned and saw Amy watching me. "What?" I asked.

She shrugged, her red hair catching the sun. "Nothing," she said. "Why don't we walk them a bit?"

"What about Cole?" Do this without Cole?

"He'll catch up," she assured me. "Come on. Just tap Mystic's sides slightly with your heels and she'll go."

I did and was surprised at how fast Mystic started moving.

"Pull back a bit and she'll slow down," Amy said. "'Whoa' works too."

"You really do say whoa?" I asked, and Mystic stopped, her ears flicking.

Amy chuckled. "You really do."

So we went, very slowly, down a road curving off around the buildings, the kids ahead.

"What do you think?" Amy asked.

I flashed on Cole, all grace and masculinity. Those deep brown eyes. His smile. Not the least bit effeminate. Not "swishy" at all.

"Oh, Pop, please" came my daughter's voice in my head. *"What'd you think? Gay guys wear dresses or something?"*

"I don't know," I said. "He's not what I expected."

"She," Amy said, and I realized she was talking about the horse, not Cole. I blushed and hoped she wouldn't notice.

"I'll tell you in a bit," I said.

It wasn't long before Cole was at our side. He was riding a lovely dark brown horse with a black mane. "Look at you, Big Daddy!" Cole's smile put his website photo to shame.

I tried to smile.

"Looking fine. Now remember, Mystic is a good horse. I can ride her without even using the reins. Just a little pressure with your legs to one side or another, and she'll move. Amy, you ride ahead. Right now, we've got Neil and Mystic blocked in."

"You got it," she said, and with a slight kick of her heels and a clucking sound, she and Galavant moved off.

I looked after her and didn't know if I wanted her to stay or was relieved she'd gone ahead. I was feeling like such a total incompetent and didn't want her to witness me doing anything stupid.

Not that I wanted to do anything stupid in front of Cole.

But then looking at him I somehow felt as if it would be okay. There was no judgment in this young man. He was too kind. I felt a twinge of guilt.

"Now put a little pressure on her right side."

I tried it, and Mystic immediately started turning to the right. "Whoa!" I said in surprise, and when she came to a sudden stop, I realized she had responded once again.

"See what a good girl she is?" Cole stated.

I nodded. Yes. But I could hardly think of her as a "girl." She was more than that.

"Do you have a hat?" Cole asked me.

"No," I said. I hated them. My hair was nothing but a mop, and no cut could control it. I looked like an idiot with my hair as short as Cole's, and if I wore a baseball cap, in no time at all I had hat hair from hell.

"We're going to have to get you something or you'll be burned up by the end of the week."

I sighed. "Okay."

"I'd loan you one of mine, but I can see your head is bigger. You must be a lot smarter than me."

"Em said I had a thick skull," I said.

"Em?"

"My wife—" My throat caught. "She's... she passed away two years ago," I explained, then wondered why. It was none of his business.

"I'm sorry," Cole said.

I nodded.

"Neil?"

I turned to him.

"Really. I am."

I looked into his face and saw those eyes, usually filled with mirth, now deep with sincerity, and saw he did mean it. "I—" My throat almost caught again. "Thank you."

He nodded. "Now what do you say we ride?"

"Okay."

"A little kick with your heels. It doesn't take much," he said.

And we were off.

Mostly.

For some reason, I kept making Mystic stop, and I wasn't sure how.

"When you turn her reins," Cole said, "you're pulling back."

"I am?" It didn't feel like it.

"Keep your hand lower. Almost rest it there at her mane. And try not to grip the saddle horn. No need to white knuckle it, Big Daddy."

I blushed again.

"You're doing fine," he said. "Rest your left hand on your thigh. Yeah, that's right. You are right-handed?"

"Yes," I said, trying not to sound terrified.

"Neil?"

I dared a look at Cole.

"You're doing great."

"Really?"

"*Really*," he assured me. "I mean it. I wouldn't lie. The only time Mystic ever dumped anyone was because the riders were assholes. You're not an asshole. She knows. Trust me, okay?"

I glanced at him.

"Do you trust me?"

Did I?

Did I have any reason *not* to?

"Okay."

"You do, don't you?"

"What?"

"Trust me?"

"I—I think I do."

"I'm glad," Cole said. "I trust you. And so does Mystic."

"She does?" I felt like a little boy who had just been praised. It felt nice.

"She's looking at you, you know."

"She is?" I looked at her, and she seemed to be looking straight ahead, although I could see the edge of one of her eyes.

"Yep, she can see you."

I checked again and... was she? *Why, she might be*, I thought. Her ears turned.

"You can tell what she's paying attention to by watching her ears, and she's paying attention to us right now."

"Gosh," I said. "Is that true, Mystic?" I asked her, and she let out the classic sound all horses make in the movies. Not the neighing, but the gentler sound. A blowing of air.

"Whickering," Cole told me.

"Wow!" I couldn't help saying.

Cole laughed.

I joined him. It felt good. Felt good to laugh, and it felt good to ride this magical animal, and it... I. I felt good.

We rode in silence for a while, and I found myself relaxing more and more. I was no longer worried so much about embarrassing myself in front of this young man. In fact, I found myself wanting to impress him.

"What kind of horse did you say she was?" I asked.

"She's an American Saddlebred," he replied.

I nodded. One type was as good as any for me. I was just trying to make conversation and calm down.

"Look around. You don't have to stare at her. Mystic will take care of you. Don't miss the countryside. Seeing the world from the back of a horse is special. There's nothing like it."

I braved it and… smiled.

The countryside was beautiful. The trees and rolling grass, the smells on the breeze, the big yellow-and-black butterflies, the sound of birdsong. Beautiful. I missed a lot in my concrete-and-brick jungle. Cole saw this every day. This was his life. What would that be like?

But more.

Cole was right.

The difference was from where I was seeing it all. There *was* nothing like it. Sitting so high on top of this animal was like nothing I'd experienced before. The closest was maybe a motorcycle ride. "It's almost like floating," I said.

"Wait until you're ready to really go. It's like flying." Cole was smiling his wide smile again, and I felt my heart skip.

"I don't think I'm quite ready to fly," I said.

"We have all week to get into mischief," he said and gave me a big wink.

I felt my stomach leap. What did he mean? I searched for a way to change the subject. "How old is she?" I asked.

"She turned eleven this year," Cole answered.

"Eleven, huh? How old are they before you can ride them?"

"We prefer three around here," he said. "If the rider is small, it can be two."

I nodded, not sure what to think of the information. I didn't know a thing about horses. Cole could have told me she was twenty-one or forty-one and that horses had to be seventeen and three-quarters and I might have believed him.

"There's your family," Cole said.

Sure enough, Amy, Crystal, Robin, and Todd were just ahead, their horses drinking from a stream. Mystic sped up, and I pulled back. She didn't want to stop, but she did slow down. I guess the instinct for water was universal.

When we reached them, Cole climbed down off his horse—it occurred to me it was the one animal whose name I didn't know; I would have to rectify that—and began checking the horses' hooves. All of them.

While he was busy with the kids, Amy rode up to me. "What do you think now?" she asked, her smile a little strange.

"Of what?" It was a big question.

"Of everything." She gestured around us. "This countryside?"

I smiled. "It's very pretty. Peaceful."

She rubbed Galavant's neck. "And the horses?"

"I'm getting used to it."

Amy cocked one eyebrow, and I felt my smile broaden.

"All right," I relented. "They're amazing."

As if making some kind of comment, Mystic chose then to make that horse noise again. I got goose bumps, and I didn't even know why. It was like magic.

"Her," I said. "I'm getting used to *her*."

"And Cole?"

My stomach dropped, and I looked over at the handsome young man. He was laughing along with our kids. "What about him?"

Why was he making me feel this way?

"Didn't I say he was a nice young man?"

I shrugged. "Sure."

Amy shook her head.

"What?" I almost barked.

"You two sure seem to be getting along fine."

What was that supposed to mean?

"Why can't you admit you like him?"

"Fine," I snapped. "I like him." My stomach began to flutter, and I couldn't help but look over at him again.

"Does it *really* bother you he's gay?" Amy asked.

"I don't understand it."

She gave me that strange look again, and I didn't like it. "Do you need to understand?"

"What do you mean?" I asked.

"Do you need to understand why he's gay? Why anyone is?"

"Pop, it's the way it is." It was my daughter's voice again. *"Some people are gay. They can't help it."*

I sighed.

"You all ready to get going?" Cole asked.

The kids cried out enthusiastically, and soon we were back on the trail, Cole at my side again.

"Mind if I ask you a question, Mr. Baxter?" he said after a bit.

I shrugged. "No."

"How old are you?"

"How old am I?" Now why did he want to know?

"Trying to do the math—not my strong point, by the way. Crystal's eighteen, and unless you started awfully early, you had to be at least that when she was born. Which would make you...."

"I'm forty-five," I said before he could continue.

He whistled. "You sure as shit don't look it. I'd have put you at thirty-eight at most."

I felt my cheeks heat up. He kept doing that to me. "Why, um, thanks. You really think so?"

"You're a good-looking man, Mr. Baxter."

"So are you," I said, then fought back a little gasp. I couldn't believe I'd said that. *Now why in the hell did you say that? Now he's going to think you're hot for him.*

Aren't you?

I cast the thought away and looked at Amy. She was looking rigidly forward, her face devoid of expression. What the hell was she thinking?

When I glanced back at Cole, he was anything but expressionless. He had a big smile on his face.

I closed my eyes—*great. Just great*—and opened them again. "Amy?"

She turned, a tiny smile on her face.

Was I the most socially incompetent person on Earth?

"Yes, babe?" Amy called.

Babe. I started at that word. *Babe?* It was the name she'd always used for Owen. Had she even realized she'd used it? Maybe it was a slip of the tongue, being here in this place, this place that she'd gone to for so many years with her husband.

I forced myself to talk. "You having a good time?"

"I am, Neil. I really am." But a tear came to her eye.

"Are you sure?" I asked, concerned.

The tear began to roll down her cheek. She nodded, wiped it away, then looked at her wet finger as if she didn't know how it had gotten that way. "Yes," she said. "I feel better than I have in a long time."

Somehow those words did something to me. I knew what she meant. Was it this place? Because despite the feelings all this had brought to the surface, I felt better as well.

And after that, I sort of lost track of time.

It was a lovely day.

Who knew riding a horse in the middle of nowhere could be so peaceful? So powerful?

Soon I found I didn't care if the day ever ended.

CHAPTER 5
Consolations

"MR. BAXTER?"

We had just gotten back from our ride and were grabbing a refreshing drink to help with the heat of the day and the dust of the road. That dust was everywhere. Even in my throat. The iced tea was heavenly.

"Mr. Baxter?"

I turned to find Darla Clark with what might have been concern on her face. But I was feeling pretty good, and I wasn't worried in the least.

"Yes, Mrs. Clark?" I said.

"Darla, please," she said.

"Only if you call me Neil."

She gave a slight shrug. "I can try. But a twenty-year habit is hard to break."

"I can't be the first guest to ask you to call them by their first name?"

She smiled. "See what I mean?"

"What is it, Darla?"

Her smile diminished. "It's about your accommodations."

"Oh?" *What about them,* I wondered. Had they still not solved whatever the problem was?

"Well," Darla said, "the Radcliffs have always used the same cabin. It's one of the family units. Two bedrooms. Mr. and Mrs. Radcliff took one room, the girls the second, and Todd slept on the foldout couch. I'm embarrassed, but we weren't thinking. The cabins have been assigned for months. Most of our reservations are. In our defense, we weren't expecting you until about a couple of weeks ago. When we thought it was going to be just her and the kids, we were either going to credit Mrs. Radcliff or give her money back. Are you seeing the problem?"

Problem? What problem? I could only blink at her.

"There's no space for you," she said. "Not enough beds."

Then I saw it. I couldn't sleep with Amy. "What about the foldout?"

"Not enough room for you and Todd, I'm afraid. It's pretty small."

"You don't have a place to put me?" I asked. No place to sleep? Then, strangely, it didn't concern me. I was in such a good space that nothing seemed to bother me. There was always the car.

"Well, actually," Darla said, scratching behind her ear, "we *do* have a solution. One I hope isn't inconvenient."

"Tell me," I said, curious.

"Well, we have a small cabin set apart from the rest, a little more private. It's about a ten-minute walk down the stream. It's very nice. Quite a step up in many ways."

"Okay," I said with a shrug, and meant it. I was feeling too good. *What, me worry?* as Alfred E. Neuman used to say.

"You haven't seen it," Darla said. "Don't you think you should see it first?"

"Okay," I repeated. Why not?

Darla nodded. "Cole will show it to you."

Cole had a big grin on his face. "Let's go, Mr. Baxter," he said, and motioning for me, he started down the porch steps. My eyes fell to the rear of his pants. Those jeans encased possibly the roundest, highest, tightest-looking butt I'd seen in a millennium. What was the saying? An ass that sticks out far enough you could set a cup of tea down on it without spilling it?

Geez, could they be much tighter?

And what are you doing looking at his butt?

I followed Cole down the steps and, despite myself, found it hard not to stare at his ass…. It, like the rest of him, looked very muscular. It flexed as he moved, and I wondered what it looked like without his jeans. Would it still be that round? Would it be smooth? Hairy? Somewhere in between?

Damn. One afternoon with a homosexual and I'm letting a lifetime of discipline slip? One afternoon and I'm imagining a man's *bare ass?*

I knew it was a mistake to have Cole as our wrangler. No. I would not allow myself to fall back onto that path. This was too good a day. I would not let perverted thoughts ruin such a perfect day.

We went around the building, and Cole indicated a golf cart with my luggage already in the back. I wondered if I was being given a choice.

Cole and I climbed aboard, and he grinned again. "Trust me, Big Daddy. You're going to love it."

Then we were zipping down the main road, past all the buildings. After a short jog, Cole turned down a path that looked like it might be too narrow. Cole was pretty confident, though; he barely slowed as we went down a fairly steep hill.

This is *a bit out of the way, isn't it?* We broke into a clearing dominated by a small, rustic-looking log cabin. It looked like something I might have constructed out of Lincoln Logs when I was a boy. It even had a green roof, although that was because grass and some other small plants were growing on it. The cabin seemed to have one end sticking right out of the side of the hill.

"Gosh," I said. It looked primitive, although it was pretty.

"Wait until you see the inside," Cole said with glee.

He jumped down, grabbed my bags, and led me onto a small porch, complete with two rocking chairs. Cole turned to me with a huge grin. "We've turned this into the newlywed cabin."

"People go on their honeymoons at a *dude* ranch?" I asked.

"They've gotten married here," he said happily and let us into the cabin.

"Whoa!" I exclaimed.

The inside was nothing like the exterior. As if in imitation of the main hall, the walls were all done in pine paneling with pretty prints, and a small version of the main hall's stone fireplace dominated the back of the room. There was a large four-poster bed on one wall, with matching bedside tables. A love seat and recliner sat by the hearth, along with a coffee table. There was even a small sink, refrigerator, and a microwave. The painting over the fireplace was of a great sleeping bear.

I didn't know whether to laugh or not about the rifle over that. So Western. The room was like a set from a Clint Eastwood movie. At least the gun seemed to have a lock. People might honeymoon at Black Bear Guest Ranch, but I was sure ugly fights happened too, like anywhere else.

"Like?" Cole asked.

I nodded, knowing he meant the cabin and not the rifle.

"I knew you would." He tossed my bags on the hope chest at the foot of the bed. "Check this out," he said and led me through a door into a striking slate bathroom with a large shower. It was easily big enough for two people.

Two men, even, I thought—and then banished the image.

"Nice, huh?" Cole asked.

"Very," I answered.

"No bathtub, but look at this!"

"This" turned out to be a backyard of sorts with a small bubbling hot tub.

"Voilà!" he exclaimed. He pointed above the hot tub. "It's protected by the roof overhang. And it's totally private." He swept his arm outward.

Indeed, the small grassy area was fenced in and ingeniously built over a creek that flowed through the backyard. "Even if someone hiked down the creek, they couldn't see you back here. The fence is too high."

He stepped close to me. "You can get naked," he said quietly. He pronounced the word "nekkid." Then: "I hate hot-tubbing with something on, don't you?"

I could only gulp.

Cole stepped even closer. "You've got this whole place to yourself. If you want to be by yourself, that is. If not, I could come keep you company."

I stood back.

Shit!

Cole was hitting on me!

And why not? The way you've practically been drooling over him.

No, I haven't!

I had to nip this in the bud now. If I had given him the wrong impression, it was time to set things right. I crossed my arms over my chest. "Cole, I am not homosexual."

A look crossed his face that would have been comical if I hadn't felt insulted. "Y-you're not?"

"No, Cole. I'm not," I said with all the strength I could muster.

"But...."

"But what?"

He shook his head and looked away. "God... I... I'm sorry."

"You thought I was homosexual." It was a statement, not a question.

Cole backed up. "I'm really sorry, Mr. Baxter."

Mr. Baxter? So I'm no longer Big Daddy? "What made you think I was gay?"

You know why he thought it!

"Because I was nice to you? Paid you a compliment? Do I *look* gay? Do I act gay?" I asked.

Did I? Had Cole been able to see something in me? How?

Cole's eyes changed then. Went hard. It was like a door slammed shut, and the light in those eyes of his winked out. He shook his head. "Do *I* look gay?" he replied. "Do *I* act it?"

"You do when you come on to me two or three hours after we meet," I said, letting my disgust show in my voice. Suddenly, his confusion was pissing me off. So I'd told him he was good-looking. So what? It didn't mean I wanted to fuck him.

Are you sure?

Once again I pushed that voice away, getting even angrier. "You're all like that, aren't you?"

Something happened to his face. It grew even harder. The play and the merriment were gone. I didn't like this new face of his. "Like what, Mr. Baxter?" he said, his voice like ice.

I gulped. Was he getting indignant? How dare he? "It's sex with you all. That's all you want. All you do!"

"We all?" His voice was even colder, if possible.

"*Gays*," I said, feeling a rise of self-righteousness. "With those clubs and bathhouses and… and AIDS."

Cole opened his mouth and then it snapped shut.

Time stopped.

"I do *not* have AIDS, Mr. Baxter. I haven't been with a man in two years. And I've been tested. Regularly. Trust me."

Yeah, right, I thought. *Trust you? Why should I trust you?* "You expect me to believe that?" And yet, inexplicably, another part of my mind was shouting something else. Asking me what the hell I was doing. That I had trusted him. He'd asked me that very question a half-dozen times today. Asked if I trusted him. And I had. Everything had been so wonderful. I'd been having the best day I'd had in a very long time.

And now?

Why, everything seemed to be going *right* to hell!

"I don't care what you believe," he replied. "It's true."

True? What was true? That he didn't have AIDS, or that he hadn't been with another man in two years?

Two years….

The same amount of time as….

How could it have been two years since he'd had sex? I'd read the articles. I'd read *Everything You Always Wanted to Know About Sex (But Were Afraid to Ask)*. I'd snuck my mother's copy and read it with a flashlight under the covers the way most guys my age read comic books, or looked at *Penthouse* and jerked off. But what I'd read horrified me instead of got me off. That chapter on homosexuality was all about how promiscuous gay men were always looking for the next cock to suck. The next man to fuck them.

If that wasn't true…. "Then what's this about?" I asked, waving back and forth between us. "You say you haven't been with anyone in two years, but you come on to me, someone you've just met? What was all this 'you can get naked in the hot tub and I'll keep you company' business?"

Cole's mouth did that open-and-shut thing again, and the ice seemed to melt. Something else took over. He looked sad.

"I-I don't know, Mr. Baxter." He looked away. "I'm sorry. It's just…. There was something… I mean… I looked at you and… I thought you were…." He stopped, turned back to me, but didn't meet my eyes. "I thought you wanted…." He stopped again. Cole visibly swallowed. "I made a mistake, Mr. Baxter. I'll leave. If you need to talk to Mrs. Clark, I'll understand." He turned and walked away, leaving me standing there. Alone.

To my surprise, I realized I didn't want him to leave. One minute I was angry and incensed, and the next I was feeling his absence like a newly missing tooth, and he wasn't even gone yet.

I had no idea why.

"Cole?" My mouth froze up before I could say anything more.

Say something! But what?

He stopped. "Yes?" he replied, his back—his broad muscular back—to me.

And what did I say? "We can be friends," I offered weakly.

"Sure," he said, then left without another word.

"Cole?" I whispered to the air.

He was gone.

I felt it. I could actually *feel* the lack of his presence.

Shit.

What was happening to me?

DINNER WAS beyond belief. I could only hope every meal wouldn't be like it or I'd gain twenty pounds, and no amount of "working ranch" would keep it off of me.

We had a Cornish hen apiece, *plus* stuffing to die for—

"The herbs were picked here in the last day or so," Amy told me.

—country-style mashed potatoes and gravy, with bits of peeling mixed in, like my grandmother used to do, green beans—

"They grow those here as well?" I asked, and Amy nodded.

—with chunks of ham, and cinnamon rolls the size of a saucer, covered in butter and crunchy goodness and still warm from the oven.

I avoided looking at Cole. At least in the eye. In the time since he'd left my cabin, I'd played the scene over and over and over in my mind. Guilt, that old enemy of mine, had hit with a vengeance. I only went to dinner reluctantly, sure I wouldn't be able to eat.

But the Black Bear Guest Ranch's food worked its superpowers on me, and I couldn't resist. Especially when Cole was so bright and cheerful, as if I had never said the things I said to him.

Then Darla Clark stood on a little stage, welcomed us again, and gave us a rundown of our schedule for the week.

Next was the entertainment.

Leo, the pudgy kid with the luggage cart, was first. Seemed he was an amateur ventriloquist, and despite the corny jokes, he had us in stitches.

"Hey Ernie," Leo asked his dummy, which was widemouthed and cue-ball bald, "if an athlete gets athlete's foot, what does an astronaut get?"

"Why, missile toe!" Ernie responded, rolling his eyes upward.

To his credit, Leo's mouth moved hardly at all. And further to his credit, people laughed.

"If a room is full of married couples, why is it still empty?" came another of Leo's jokes.

Now Ernie's eyes moved back and forth, as if looking around the room. "Because there isn't a single person in it."

More laughter. Especially the kids, who I wasn't convinced got the joke. I think they just liked the comical movement of those big eyes.

"How do you know carrots are good for your eyes?"

"Because you never see rabbits wearing glasses!"

This time the kids *did* laugh. They squealed in delight. That one they got.

"Why did the man sleep under the car?"

"So he could wake up oily in the morning."

And so on.

Even I laughed, although the jokes were pretty simple. But this was a family place. Dirty jokes wouldn't be appropriate, and the one about the married couples was about as racy as he got. The laughter felt good and relieved the tension from my incident with Cole. I'd avoided looking at him during the meal but dared look now. He was laughing at the jokes he'd surely heard dozens of times before, and his laughter was contagious. Those eyes of his, that mouth, lit up the table. I had to keep myself from staring.

Gay.

He was *gay*. He was *proudly* gay. He was *indignantly* gay! I looked around and saw several women staring at him. His looks spared no age as a girl of no more than thirteen or fourteen and a woman old enough to be Darla's mother were all but ogling him. The old lady was even waving and giggling.

Cole could have almost any woman he wanted. I even caught Amy giving him a long, appreciative look. Why would he choose men when he so obviously could be with women? Did he want to have a life where he was ostracized? Hated? Sneered at? A life where he was unable to have a romantic dinner with his lover (lover!) without people staring or pointing or even threatening him? Didn't he want a normal life? Stability? Acceptance? A wife and home and children?

My daughter claimed that some people were just gay. Like she would know. Eighteen and she thought she knew everything. *"Pop, it's the way it is."* She said some people couldn't help it. But I didn't believe it. I couldn't believe it.

Cole *did* have a choice.

I believed *that*.

I *had* to!

Or had the more liberal and indulgent culture that had arisen since I was Cole's age seduced him into thinking otherwise?

Unbidden, an image of Jack, a friend from high school, came to mind. And George. Oh, George too—

Hey, Neil, do you ever play with it?

—and I pushed their memories away.

When Leo was done, a small group took the stage—including Cassie, the curly-headed blonde wrangler—and did a couple of square dance routines. Darla's husband, Vincent, played a mean fiddle, calling out moves while he did so.

"Now, 'member, folks," he said gleefully between numbers, "to pay attention. Cuz y'all are doin' this Tuesday night!"

My eyes went wide. Had Darla mentioned square dancing? How had I missed that? Nightmares of elementary school and me messing up and the kids making fun of me rushed back.

First horseback riding and now this?

Was this place designed to torture me?

Of course, riding Mystic hadn't been as bad as I'd thought it would be. In fact, it had been wonderful.

But square dancing? That was something else again!

I looked to Amy, who laughed, then reached out and took my hand. "You'll be fine," she said loudly to be heard over Vincent's resumed fiddling. "You'll have fun. I'll protect you."

When Vincent and his group finished, our wranglers brought out dessert.

"But we had those cinnamon buns," I protested, but I shut up when I saw what Cole had brought. It was huge pieces of pie, our choice of apple or pecan.

"Let me guess," I said. "Grown on the ranch?"

"Sure is!" Cole said. He gave me a strange, quirky smile and refused to meet my eyes. "Both the apples and the pecans. And we've got home-churned vanilla ice cream."

After one bite, I knew I'd never get in my jeans by next Sunday. I couldn't say no. It was all just too enticing. Delicious beyond words. We dug in, but to my surprise, Cole didn't join us. He let Leo take over our table, and Cole headed for the stage.

That's when I saw Cole had a guitar. Where had it come from? He sat on the edge of a stool, propped one booted heel on a rung, fussed for a second tuning his instrument… and then he began to play.

Well. Really well.

He had a nice voice too. Reminded me a bit of Michael Bublé, but a tad rougher. But kind. A weird word to use, but it fit. Kind and strong and deep. He did maybe three, four songs. That many before the next performer, but he didn't bore any of us from the expressions I saw on people's faces.

"Blackbird," by the Beatles—which struck me, because it had been a haunting favorite of mine since I'd first heard it way back in high school. Then a country song—which I am not a big fan of, but Cole made it work. Followed by the classic "Home on the Range," of all things. And finally something, he informed us, by someone named Christine Cain… or Kane? I found myself falling into the song and knew I'd have to look her up when I got home.

The lyrics drew me in.

"And all the poets taught me," he told us in song, "that there's a difference between free, and just pretending not to see."

Whoa. For some reason the words hit me hard.

"How will you go," he continued, "the long, long journey, if you're always about to begin?"

Strange song to pick for a last number, but Cole finished to a loud round of applause, which freed me from the world his singing had taken me to.

I shook my head. The lyrics had shaken me up, and I didn't even know why.

And was he looking at me as he came down from the stage?

Into me?

Afterward, I hung back a bit with Amy. And hell, keeping her company was what I was supposed to be doing in the first place. We had coffee, which I knew would keep me up, but I did it anyway. Amy loved ending an evening with her coffee. The caffeine never kept her from sleeping when she wanted to. At home, I had to make sure I had some Bailey's in mine or I'd be up half the night.

"I miss him, Neil," she said, looking around the room. "He'd have had so much fun tonight."

I had no idea what to say. There was no reason for me to ask who "he" was. I'd wondered why she wanted to come here. I wouldn't have. Couldn't, if our positions were reversed. I missed Emily—every day. And I hid from her, as much as I could. Even now. And here was Amy, facing the very ghosts I'd worried she'd have to confront. What was there to say? I still hadn't dealt with Em after two years. How could I offer sage advice for my friend when her husband had died less than two months ago?

But then I remembered that advice wasn't something I'd wanted. All I really wanted was company. I wanted someone to listen to me.

So that was what I gave Amy. My ear, and *no* advice.

"I look at Robin, and she worries me."

I nodded. I knew about Amy's worries in that department. Robin had cried for an afternoon and then seemed to bounce right back. She hadn't shown any grief since then. She was bright and positive and told everyone that she was okay.

"At least Todd is quiet. I can tell he misses Owen fiercely. He's using that whole 'now I'm the man of the house' to get through. I want to tell him to fuck that. To cry. To really cry! Or at least, I did. A few weeks ago I was passing his room on my way to the kitchen to get some water one night, and I heard him crying. For a minute I almost knocked on the door, but then the relief—the pure relief that he at least was letting it out—stopped me from doing it. That and the fact that being the man of the house is so important to him."

She went silent.

Then she talked about the first time they came here. Owen was a huge Western fan—had read the books by Louis L'Amour, Zane Grey, and Max Brand since he was a kid. He loved the movies, too, and had infected both Todd and Robin.

Amy gave me a laugh. It was a little one, but a laugh all the same. "Robin was like you at first," Amy told me. "Not so excited about bugs and dust and the heat."

But it was the horses that drew her in. She was the little girl who always wanted a pony.

"I hadn't been all that excited either, but Owen never expressed a preference for any of our vacations—not once. So who was I to say no? As it turned out, we all had a wonderful time, even the night we slept on the ground, learning what it was like to rough it like in the Old West."

She smiled, her eyes going to a far different time and place.

"We went back the very next year, and brought Crystal, as you know, and continued every year after that."

She looked at me, her eyes coming back to the present. Sighed. She smiled, but I could tell it was forced. "This just might be the very last year," she said. She shrugged. "I don't know if I'll want to come back after I say...." Her voice faded again. "Good-bye."

It didn't take long after that for her to decide she was ready to turn in.

"Want me to walk you?" I asked as we stepped out onto the porch.

She shook her head. "No. I think I want a few minutes to be alone before facing the kids." She kissed my cheek, thanked me for coming, and headed into the night.

Unexpectedly, I found Cole and Leo leaning against my golf cart, and it looked like they were passing a flask. I cleared my throat, and they spun, obviously surprised at being caught.

"Good night, Leo," Cole said.

Leo looked at Cole, me, then back at Cole.

Oh, for goodness sake, I thought, recognizing Leo's expression almost instantly. Women had been giving Cole that very same look all evening.

Shit.

Leo too?

"Go on," Cole said.

The shorter boy looked stricken and turned to me, nodded, then ran off into the night.

"Did I interrupt something?" I asked.

Cole shrugged. "He's got a crush on me."

I felt my stomach clench. "Maybe I should've been the one to get lost," I said, trying to be casual. Had I stopped some homosexual liaison?

Cole shook his head. "He's not my type.... Too young."

"How old is he?" *Eighteen, maybe?* Was Cole giving liquor to a minor?

"He's twenty-one," Cole answered.

"He is?" I was surprised. "He sure doesn't look it."

"Nope, and that's the problem. He's a nice guy. He'll make some guy a great lover one day. But I can't be attracted to someone who I'm not attracted to, you know?"

I guess I had assumed differently. Had I thought all a gay man needed from his partner for the evening was a penis? Maybe I had. Probably.

"I imagine you'd like someone a little closer to your age? Em and I were only a few months apart in—"

"I like older men," Cole said and looked away.

Older men? How old? Older as in.... My stomach fluttered, and I refused to let my thoughts go where his words threatened to take me. I needed to change the subject. Fast.

"You were good in there," I told him. After all, it was true.

He looked at me, those dark eyes all but lost in the shadows of the porch. "Thanks."

"You're welcome."

We stood there for a minute, neither of us saying anything.

The conversation we had earlier—the very ugly one—began to play in my mind again. The guilt came back. I looked away.

I need to get to my cabin. I need to get out of here.

Now.

Cabin. Sleep. But, hell, I was going to be up for hours. I could feel the caffeine zinging through me like electricity. Maybe the hot tub? But that reminded me of Cole's little pass.

Shit.

Cole looked away again, started to take a drink from his flask, then stopped. "Want some?"

"What is it?" I asked.

"Does it matter?" he replied and laughed.

I shrugged. "I guess not." *Hell*, I thought, *it might help me sleep.* I reached for the flask, and when he handed it to me, our fingers touched for a second.

I almost jumped.

It was like one of those static zings that happens when you rub your stockinged feet on a carpet and then touch something metal. But that wasn't what happened. There hadn't been a static discharge. It had all been in my imagination. In my head.

But then when he looked at me the way he did, shadows or not, I wondered if that was true.

I paused for a moment before drinking, the fear of AIDS suddenly rising to the surface like noxious swamp gas. And then something I did know about the virus rose upward as well. Even if Cole did have AIDS, I couldn't get it by drinking out of the flask.

I looked at Cole.

Beautiful Cole.

Beautiful?

I trembled. Geez. Yes. He was beautiful.

"I do not have AIDS, Mr. Baxter," he had told me. *"I haven't been with a man in two years. And I've been tested. Regularly. Trust me."*

I wanted to trust him.

With an uncomfortable abruptness, I remembered the hateful words of the guys from the dock I worked during the summers between my high school years.

"Never pass a bottle with a queer. You might as well kiss the buttfucker. Think where his goddamned lips have been! Sucking cock for one thing. Eating some shit-covered ass! Fucking death-germs, man! It's no wonder they all got AIDS."

"I do not have AIDS, Mr. Baxter. I haven't been with a man in two years."

Dammit!

Was I being like those hateful, ugly people?

I looked into Cole's eyes and suddenly realized I *was*. I was being *just* as bad as they were. Gay or not, Cole had shown me nothing but kindness.

"Do you trust me?" he'd asked when I rode Mystic. When he'd told me that Mystic trusted me.

Agree with what he'd decided to do with his life or not, he'd done nothing but been trustworthy.

Fuck!

I was so ignorant. I didn't know anything. Why wasn't I better educated? No, I hadn't been in the "sex pool" in a very long time. But I had a daughter old enough to be having sex, after all. I should know about these things. And as uncomfortable as that idea made me, it was one I needed to deal with. And damn! How was that even possible? That she was eighteen? When did that happen? I somehow still felt her age.

And also like I was at least a hundred years old. Two hundred. More…. Had Crystal been through some of what I had been through? It was possible. She probably knew more about condoms than I did. Was she a virgin? I hated this. I hated the way my thoughts seemed to be swinging in a hundred directions.

I took a swig from the flask, knowing those lips had touched it before mine, and felt the burn. "Whiskey." I handed it back.

"*Good* Kentucky whiskey," he said, then took a drink. He held it out.

I took the flask and, once again, our fingers touched. He didn't let go for a second, letting the contact linger. I didn't pull away, and my heart began to race.

He was flirting again.

Dammit!

Why me?

He let go, and I took a long swallow this time. Too long. *Shit.* "I think I finished it," I said. "I'm sorry."

"I got plenty back at my cabin," he said. "Don't worry about it."

Was that an invitation?

Damn, he was so good-looking! Hell! How could a man be so damned good-looking? He was a man! Why was I seeing it? Weren't there plenty of nice-looking women around here? But when I tried to think, nothing but the old lady that had been ogling Cole came to mind. And Charlize Theron she wasn't. Why couldn't I think of one single attractive woman? Out of thirty-some people, there had to be one. Besides Amy, that was. Amy was family. Amy was my "sister."

Again, we just stood there, and I felt the heat in my face as I went all flush.

Go to bed! my mind screamed at me. *Get out of here!*

But why couldn't I move?

"My flask?" he asked.

"Sorry," I said, feeling like an idiot. I handed it to him. "I need to be getting to bed. I'm worn out. It was a long drive, and all that food and the horse...."

I paused.

Remembered.

I looked at Cole again, but this time I could think of something besides how attractive he was. I remembered the amazing afternoon astride that incredible animal. How free I'd felt. How spellbinding. "Thank you for that."

"For what?" Cole said.

"Mystic. It was magical."

He smiled, and my stomach leapt again.

Get out of here!

"No problem," he said. "There'll be plenty more tomorrow. You rest up. I'll see you in the morning."

"Morning" was all I could say back.

Then he turned—

"Cole?"

—and stopped.

"Yes, Mr. Baxter?"

I said it before I even knew I was going to. "I'm sorry. About what I said."

"I don't know what you're talking about," he said and walked off.

I watched him go.

And finally I climbed into my little cart and drove back to my cabin.

I COULDN'T sleep. All I could think about was Cole. His eyes, his grin, the touch of his fingers when we passed the flask.

Shit.

A lifetime of control flying out the window in a single day. Not *even* a day.

I like older men.

My stomach was full of butterflies. Did he mean me?

I haven't been with a man in two years.

Really? He hadn't? Why? A man as nice-looking—*hot! He's hot!*—as Cole could get any man—gay man—he wanted.

Were his reasons anything like mine?

No.

Of course not.

I looked at you and... I thought you were....

He thought I was what? Homosexual? Of course he did. All he had to do was look at me and I acted like a twelve-year-old girl.

I got up. Paced. This was crazy. I was never going to get to sleep. *Damned coffee.*

It wasn't the coffee, though.

If only I had drunk more of his whiskey.

That made me think of fingertips again. And the fact his lips had been on the flask....

Shit! I *was* acting like a teenage girl! I was a man. A grown man!

I went to the cabinet over the sink to see if there was a glass for water.

There was a half bottle of whiskey. I took it out. Jim Beam Choice (green label)? Cole's? *Good* Kentucky whiskey?

Mine tonight.

I screwed off the cap and took a long, hard drink, my throat working to swallow the wild, bitter taste. The whiskey exploded in my belly and intense heat spread through me.

One or two more of these and I'll sleep like a baby.

I did.

More or less.

CHAPTER 6
Naked

I WOKE up with a start, not knowing for a moment where I was. It was the birds that had awakened me. I could hear them chattering and singing, and I rose naked from the bed.

Hmmm.... I usually wore boxers to bed, at least. *How much did I drink last night?* I didn't feel hung over, so it mustn't have been too much.

The alarm clock read just after seven thirty, and I thought it was at least nine before we were scheduled to do anything. I had an hour and a half to kill.

I found my jeans on the floor by the kitchen sink—*how had they gotten there?*—and my underwear in the bathroom. I put them both on and walked barefoot out onto the porch. Something buzzed by my face, and when I looked around, I saw two hummingbirds at a feeder, their throats glowing ruby red in the morning sunlight. The tiny creatures were hovering midair, and the sight took my breath away. I'd never seen hummingbirds so close before, and as a third one joined them, I could actually see it had a glistening green throat. I stepped closer, and they shot away, one seeming to scold me as it did so. I couldn't help but laugh in delight.

It was a stunning morning.

Coffee. Sit on the porch and drink coffee, I thought. Did I have a coffeemaker in the cabin?

My thoughts were interrupted by the sound of a horse, and soon I saw it wasn't one, but two. Cole sat atop his horse, and he was leading Mystic.

"You're up," he said. "Good morning!"

I suddenly realized I wasn't wearing a shirt and Cole was looking at me. Not rudely or anything, but looking all the same.

Once again, Cole made me blush.

"Morning," I said and crossed my arms over my chest. I felt so exposed. But why? I had pants on. What was the big deal? I'd been around men when I wasn't wearing a shirt all my life.

But were they looking at you like that?

"I come bearing coffee and bagels," he said, holding up a Thermos and a brown paper bag.

He brought me breakfast.

"Let me get a shirt," I said before I headed back inside.

"Bring a mug," he called after me.

I pulled a shirt from the duffel bag I still hadn't unpacked. The baggiest T-shirt I had. I found a coffee mug next to the sink and went back out. Cole was sitting in one of the rockers and pouring steaming coffee into the red lid of his Thermos. It smelled wonderful. He held it out as if to pour, and I offered my mug. I noticed it had a bear on it, of course.

"Cream? Sweetener?"

"No, thanks," I said and sat down next to him.

Cole was wearing tight jeans again, a pale blue cowboy shirt— the top few snaps were undone, and I could see his chest looked totally smooth. Would he have a few stray hairs tucked between his pecs or surrounding his nipples? His black cowboy hat was perched slightly forward on his head.

I looked away and saw he'd tied the horses to a railing set away from the porch. Mystic was pulling at some grass.

I heard the bag crinkling and turned as Cole held it out for me.

I peeked in to see a large bagel and some packets of cream cheese.

"I toasted it for you, but I didn't know if you'd want anything on it," he said.

"Thanks," I replied, and after taking the bagel, I smeared it with a good two packets of the Philadelphia brand. "Something that wasn't grown or made here," I said, holding up an empty packet.

Cole laughed. "Not the bagel either. Comes from a great little shop in town."

"How far is town?" I took a huge bite of the bagel. Delicious.

"About twenty miles," Cole said. "Not far."

"I wouldn't want to walk it." I stuck out a foot and flexed my toes.

Cole pointed. "Hobbit feet!"

"Huh?" I looked down at my foot.

"Hairy on top," Cole explained. "Like a hobbit."

"Oh." I didn't know if it was a good thing or not, so I asked him.

"*I* think it's good," he replied, and his cheeks turned pink.

I followed suit and tucked my foot under the rocker—and felt naked once more. *You're only barefoot. Why the hell are you embarrassed?*

Because he likes my feet!

That's not exactly what he said.

Time for a subject change.

I took a careful drink of my coffee. Damn, it was terrific coffee. Had it been so good last night?

"It's fresh ground," Cole explained, and I realized he meant the coffee. He must have seen the appreciation on my face.

"Definitely not a commercial blend," he continued. "And no, we don't grow coffee here either." He chuckled.

"So why this?" I said, holding up the bagel and coffee.

"*Hmmm?*" he asked.

"Breakfast in… porch," I answered, then fought a blush at the connotation.

"Oh!" He rolled his eyes. "Your family's up already and eating the continental breakfast, and they asked if we could go riding this morning. Monday is usually horse orientation, but they know horses front and back, and we already covered the reminders yesterday. So I said yes, and since I already had Madrigal saddled, I went ahead and got Mystic ready for you."

"Oh! I kept trying to remember to ask you your horse's name."

Cole nodded. "I call her Maddy. Rode on down 'cause I wasn't sure when you'd be up. I need to get you a radio."

"Okay," I said. "When do I need to be up there this morning?"

"Well, we are talking about three kids," Cole answered. "So about an hour ago."

"An hour ago?" I jumped up.

"Finish," he said with a wave at my breakfast.

I sat and took another monstrous bite.

"We really do need to get you a hat," Cole replied.

I shook my head. "I never was much of a hat guy," I said through a mouthful of bagel.

"Well, you got a little sun yesterday."

"I did?" I touched my face and maybe felt a little heat there.

"You need something," Cole explained. "You'll fry."

"I guess," I said.

"At least a cap. Why don't we check the gift shop when you're done? They're pretty reasonable."

I nodded, gobbled the last of my breakfast, and went inside for my boots. I peeked in the bathroom mirror while I was there, and sure enough, my cheeks were a rosy red. Not *too* bad, though. Knowing me it would tan out by the next morning, as long as it wasn't made worse today. At least it'd cover my blushing.

Then it was time to try to get on Mystic again. Would Cole help me?

Turns out he didn't need to. I did better the second time. And when Cole swung up onto his horse, I couldn't help but notice how the muscles in his thighs and ass flexed in his skintight jeans.

I looked away.

Why? Look. What's looking going to hurt?

No! It was the first step on a slippery slope. *Do not look!*

Of course this was only Monday. How did I *not* look for the whole next week?

THE BASEBALL-STYLE caps weren't bad. They came in several different colors, and, yes, they had a bear patch on the front. They were cheap, and Cole did insist I needed one. Amy appeared in the shop and nodded her agreement as she headed over to a turnstile filled with postcards.

"You're pink today," she said over her shoulder. "You'll be a lobster by tonight."

"All right! All right!" I cried, hands raised in surrender.

"I've got something later to help with that burn," Cole said. "A cream we can put on you. The stuff is like magic."

"Sure," I mumbled while I looked at two caps. Red or black?

"Of course," Cole said, "you'd look real good in one of these." And before I knew what he was doing, he'd placed a cowboy hat on my head. "Whoa!"

"Gosh," Amy said. I turned and she was blinking at me, wide-eyed.

"What?" I asked her.

"*Grrrrrrrrrr...!*"

"Grrrr?" What was that supposed to mean?

"*Grrrrrrr* is right," Cole said with a growl of his own.

He placed those big square-tipped hands on my shoulders and turned me so I was looking into a full-length mirror. "Just look, Big Daddy."

I looked at my image in surprise. I looked pretty good. The hat— black, much like Cole's—complemented my dark eyes and hair rather well. And here I imagined I'd look stupid in a cowboy hat. I saw the look in Cole's eyes over my shoulder and felt my face heat up.

That look! He was making me feel naked again.

At least he wouldn't see I was blushing through my sunburn.

"You look great. Like a real cowboy. I mean it."

I laughed. Me? A "real" cowboy? I turned away from the mirror. "It's probably pretty expensive."

"Don't worry about it," Amy said. "Let's make it an early birthday present, babe." There was that word again, and it made me nervous.

"No, no," I said.

"When's your birthday?" Cole asked.

"In about a month," I said, glancing back at my reflection. The hat really did look good.

"Well, happy early birthday, Daddy," Cole said.

I like older men. The memory of his words almost made me blush again. *How much older?* I wondered.

"I'm buying it for you," Amy insisted, and a few minutes later I stepped out into the sun in my cowboy attire.

WE RODE quite a bit that day. First on a trail, where we explored much of the ranch. Then, after a hamburger and hot dog lunch, we actually learned to herd cattle. Darla and Vincent needed about two-hundred head moved from one end of the ranch to the other. It was a little scary at first, what with those horns. I'd never been around cows in real life, except at a state fair when I was a kid visiting my grandmother, and they'd been in pens. But Cole and the other wranglers certainly knew what they were doing—and they were doing most of the work—and soon had me a little more comfortable around the large animals.

"Keep behind and off to the side," Cole instructed. "Just sorta pressure them at their hips. You hardly need touch them. They'll go, believe me."

Suddenly I was having fun "working" the ranch. I looked around me, surrounded by cattle and horses and riders, and felt a little thrill zip through me. It was like I was living some old classic Western movie. The riders were calling out, the sun was beating down, the dust was in the air. For a while, I let myself pretend I really was a cowboy, living a hundred years ago on a long cattle train.

What must that have been like? I wondered. It could only have been something vaguely like this. They had months on the trail with only the crudest tents for shelter against the elements. Storms, the heat, the cold, the filth. Beans for nearly every meal. I had huge dinners in a dining hall, a cabin to myself, a microwave, a shower, a hot tub—and oh, was that hot tub starting to call my name. My ass was hurting from the hours in the saddle, and as wonderful as Mystic was, I was getting tired.

I found it a tremendous relief when we were finally done and heading back to the stables. How had the real cowboys in those long ago days stood it? It even hurt to climb down.

I stretched, put my hands on my lower back, and felt it pop. I was going to sleep well tonight. *Note to self: no coffee tonight.*

Unless Cole was around with his flask and could add some of his whiskey.

"Anyone interested in some volleyball?" Cole called out as we put our tack away.

"Hell no," I moaned. "Count me out."

"What's wrong, Big Daddy?" Cole asked and came up behind me. "You tired? I know a big man like you isn't tired."

"You're wrong," I said. "And I'm going to jump in that hot tub and relax before dinner."

"Suit yourself," Cole replied. "We're gonna have fun!"

"Have at it," I said, heading for my golf cart. I'd been almost embarrassed by it at first, but now I was grateful for…. Then I remembered. The little electric cart was back at the cabin. Cole had brought Mystic by this morning, and I'd ridden her up, not the cart.

Shit, I thought with a groan and made my way slowly back home.

THE HOT tub was beyond wonderful. It didn't take a lot to figure out how to get the jets going, and soon I was relaxing in the steaming, churning water. I couldn't get over how quickly the massaging effect made my muscles feel so much better. Even though the roof stuck out over it to keep the weather off, if I sat at one end and lay back, I could look up into the robin's-egg-blue sky. It was so pretty and peaceful. Above a lone bird—hawk? Eagle? I didn't know—floated above me, riding the air currents. I let my body float to the water's surface and imagined how it felt to be that bird. Anything like this?

Free! No worries. No cares about what anyone else thought of it.

My toes curled, and I flexed them. It felt good. Hobbit feet, indeed! Of course, even the knuckles of my toes had hair. Geez, I *did* have hobbit feet.

Cole likes them.

While looking at the objects of Cole's attention, I noticed my bright orange trunks and laughed. They *were* ridiculous. They went to nearly my knees. What happened to smaller trunks? Whose idea were they anyway? Awful! Just awful. In college my trunks had barely covered my butt. Emily had loved them. Why did men practically wear slacks in the pool these days? Were they hiding?

Like you're hiding?

Take them off.

Be free.

You can get nekkid.

No one will see.

I had to wrestle with the idea. I'd never been naked outside in my life. Not once. Not even in the open-sky locker rooms lining the beaches on that Orlando vacation Em and I had once taken. I'd been horrified. Which Em had found hilarious.

"Who are you afraid will see you?" she'd asked. "Helicopter pilots?"

But now Cole's suggestion was in my mind, and it would not let go. Foolishly, I looked around me—there was a fence, so who was going to see me if someone wandered by?

Do it! Don't be a chickenshit. Do it. Damn. With a jolt of fear and excitement, I stood and climbed out of my practically fluorescent trunks. For a second, I held them in front of me, hiding my privacy. Then—slowly—I forced myself to drop my hands to my sides.

I was naked.

Outside.

My penis, my ass, totally and for the first time ever exposed to the world. A very small part of it. A fenced-in section of it. But exposed nevertheless.

I grinned.

It felt good, like so much else around this place.

I wanted to shout. I wanted to let out a Tarzan yell and beat on my chest and wag my not-so-privates at the sky. Why not? Maybe not yell. I didn't want anyone to come running.

But the rest?

I laid the trunks aside and raised my arms above me, threw back my head, and wiggled my sore ass. The bubbling water was right at the level to tickle my balls, and I laughed aloud.

It did.

It felt good to be naked.

To my surprise, I felt my penis stir, and when I looked, it gave a jump. *Goodness!* The watching seemed to urge it on, and my cock began to rise—as if in imitation of my arms to the sky.

I laughed again and, with a final surge, my cock rose to complete erection. *Damn!* When did just *getting* a hard-on feel so good? I hadn't even touched myself.

Yet.

When was the last time I even had an orgasm? A week? No. A month? I couldn't even remember. I'd always preferred the real thing to masturbation. The latter needed me to conjure images and there lay dragons.

I sat down.

Right into a jet that was just right—not too gentle, not too rough—to stimulate my arousal to a moan-inducing degree.

I shifted back a bit, and another gentle jet was hitting me in the tailbone, and *that* felt good too. The tailbone? I hadn't even known it was sore. I cocked my hips a tad more and the—*Oh!*—my eyes went wide. The water was hitting me someplace a couple of inches lower and even more private than my erection and—*oh, oh, oh!*—my eyes rolled up with a will of their own.

Damn! Who knew *that* could feel so good? The erotic massage was so intense. Without realizing what I was doing, I began to rock back and forth, back and forth, letting those two jets play with my straining cock and my most private place.

Goosebumps raced up my arms and across my shoulders. Could I come this way? Without touching myself?

Cole was right. Getting in a hot tub "nekkid" was better. Was this what he meant? Of course it was… or something like it. Like maybe taking him up on his invitation to join me? What would he be doing to me if he were here right now? Would he be touching me? My cock? My other place? Would he want to suck me? Cole's beautiful, sexy face filled my mind—those incredible eyes, that smile, that mouth. Unbidden, I found myself picturing him sucking me.

Fuck!

I began to moan uncontrollably, unmindful of the noise I was making—not caring. Yes, I could come this way! And I was going to. I was getting closer. Closer. Closer.

"Mr. Baxter?"

I froze, my brain slamming into a brick wall.

There was a knock on the fence. "Mr. Baxter?"

Fuck! It was Cole.

"I… I…." I tried to speak but couldn't. I'd been so close to orgasm. My testicles were shouting for release. A few more rocks against the jets would have been all it would have taken.

There was a click, and I saw the latch of the gate open—was there some kind of string to pull on the other side? Dammit!

The gate opened, and Cole was standing there.

"You okay, Mr. Baxter?"

"I… I…." I nodded. "Yes." That last word sounded as if I'd sucked on helium. I cleared my throat and laid my arms along the back of the hot tub, trying to look casual.

"I brought you some of that cream," he said, holding out a yogurt container. "It has all kinds of herbs in it—aloe, echinacea, lavender, calendula, comfrey—all mixed up in whipped vitamin E. Just don't forget and eat it."

"Herbs grown at Black Bear?" My voice was now a little bit more normal.

"Some of 'em!" Cole said proudly. "Also, I wanted to let you know they're getting ready to put the steaks on the grill for dinner. And I guarantee you they'll be the best steaks you've ever had in your life!"

"Dinner?" My voice was practically back to itself. Was it dinnertime already?

Cole nodded. "Cook let me know they were ready a little early, and we're going to go ahead and start in about twenty minutes or so, all right?"

"Sure," I said, and just exactly then the jets stopped.

Seconds later—who knew it would happen so quickly?—the foam was gone.

And that fast, Cole looked down.

To his credit, he blushed.

He turned away. "Ah…. Look. I'll leave the cream. Meet you back at the dining hall? You… finish up whatever you were doing and…. Later!"

And quick as a flash, out the gate he went.

Finish? What did he mean by…?

Finish!

Finish masturbating? The embarrassment was excruciating.

Finish by jerking off? How could I?

But how could I not? Even humiliation had done nothing to wilt my throbbing hard-on. I'd been too close to orgasm, and my balls were aching, crying out in need. I had to finish.

I grabbed myself, jacking, and immediately wondered if I *could* finish. My balls wanted it, but my mind had gone somewhere where only the most embarrassed of thoughts could go.

How could Cole have looked at my….

Because he's gay, you idiot. Wouldn't you have looked if there had been a woman in the hot tub?

I knew the answer.

No.

The answer was no.

I wouldn't have looked. I would have averted my eyes. And no need to pretend it was because I was a gentleman. I wouldn't have *wanted* to see. I'd rarely looked at Em down *there*.

That shame made me see orgasm *really* would be impossible.

Unless….

Shit!

I closed my eyes, and Cole instantly filled my mind once more. Those eyes. Those lips. I imagined him taking me in his mouth, what it would feel like, what it would look like….

And seconds later, an orgasm, exquisitely pleasurable and almost painful, hit me so hard and fast I nearly shouted. When I came down from the wave of conflicting sensations, there was only one thought in my foggy brain.

How could this be happening? So fast? A lifetime of discipline wiped away like chalk from a blackboard. Cole's mere existence had opened feelings and thoughts like water being released from the floodgates.

What was I going to do?

CHAPTER 7
Confrontations

I JOINED everyone for dinner around back of the main dining hall, where numerous picnic benches had been set up and were already crowded with people. It was easy to find my family, and Cole was there, of course; where else would he be? I tried to avert my eyes and was once again grateful for the slight sunburn on my cheeks. It would hide any of the blushing Cole could call forth with but one flick of his dark eyes.

I needn't have worried. Cole was a perfect gentleman. No knowing smile, no twinkle to his eyes. No more than usual, that was. It was like nothing had happened.

Not far from the tables was the man referred to as "Cook." He was huge, and not in girth. He was a bit wide, but what was so impressive was his pure size. I knew he was well over six feet tall, but had he topped seven? He was bald, his scalp gleaming from sweat from the sun and the heat of the grills. The hands flipping the dozens of steaks were immense.

The smell of cooking meat filled the air, and I found my mouth was watering. I was starved! And how could that be? I'd had both a cheeseburger and a hot dog for lunch.

One bite of my medium-rare steak, a huge, thick thing, and I was catapulted to heaven. It was quite simply the best steak I had ever tasted in my life, just as Cole had predicted, and my eyes rolled up in my head in ecstasy. The baked potatoes (grown on the ranch?), loaded with cheese and sour cream, were just as delicious. Everything was good, the weather was just right, the emotions light and high. Laughter and the sound of smacking lips filled my ears. The evening was ideal.

Amy sat on one side of me and Crystal on the other. She was excited about the volleyball game. Apparently, she'd been spot on with a game in which her poor skills were usually legendary.

"She kicked butt," Cole said. He was two people down from Amy and, damn, I found myself wishing he was next to me.

Crystal beamed at his praise. Cole's attention did things to everyone. "Tonight's the bonfire," Cole said. "And s'mores."

That generated a lot of enthusiasm, and I found even I was looking forward to that. I hadn't had the campfire treats since I was a kid. They were about the only thing—*except skinny-dipping with George*—I'd liked about my enforced summer church-camp days.

George. I hadn't thought of him in years.

Liar!

How long had it been? The last time I'd seen him was—

Hey, Neil, do you ever play with it?

—the summer before my freshman year in high school. I always saw him at church camp. Dreaded and longed to see him at the same time. The guilt and the longing always at war.

And how could I forget?

Because we got caught. The camp directors had threatened to call my mother. I'd begged them not to. I'd cried and cried. Told them it was all George's fault because he was two years older and talked me into it, and they believed me—because he was older and they thought me an innocent kid—and George's mother had come and taken him away.

I'd been terrified for months that my mom would find out. She almost always found out. Knowing for sure she might truly kill me that time.

And the shame! I'd been haunted by the guilt of that for years. I'd been no innocent. I'd wanted everything George wanted to do. I seduced him when it was his turn to feel guilty and to say we shouldn't be doing what we were doing. Sure, he'd started everything. Started it with those words whispered to me when we snuck out of our cabin to try a cigarette.

Hey, Neil, do you ever play with it?

I'd hated the cigarette, but I had liked what we did after that.

I never found out what happened to George. We hadn't had the chance to exchange phone numbers or anything. I wasn't sure where he was from exactly, and he'd had a perfectly boring last name, like Smith or something, so I couldn't have found him if I'd wanted to.

I'd actually briefly considered killing myself. There was a swift river near my house, and I'd even stood on the edge of it once, contemplating jumping in. A school counselor had figured out something was wrong, got me to his office, and finally dragged it out of me.

That's when he told me something that I'd held on to for a long time. He told me boys fooling around with boys was normal.

"It is?" I'd asked, stunned, heart trip-hammering in my chest.

"What was it exactly that you two did?" he asked, laying a hand on my shoulder and sitting next to me.

"We…. We…." I couldn't say it.

But the man, I couldn't remember his name—

Liar!

—used those skills of his to drag that out of me too.

I told him that we jerked off together. And that sometimes we did it to each other.

And he assured me that was perfectly normal. That I was going through all these hormonal changes and there was nothing wrong with what we'd done.

I had grabbed hold of that like a life preserver in a raging storm in the middle of an ocean, even though there was more after that and it had creeped me out, and I prayed and prayed that Mom still wouldn't find out because I knew *she* wouldn't think what we had done was normal at all.

"You okay, Neil?"

I jolted out of the memory and turned to Amy, who had a dripping ear of corn in hand with a row of kernels missing and butter smeared on her lips. "You went all pale, babe," she said.

I did? I said. Or tried to. Nothing came out. I nodded instead.

I took a drink of tea. "Fine."

"You sure?" I could see the concern on her face.

"Yeah," I somehow managed. "Sure."

"You look like you could use something a lot stronger than tea," she said. "Like maybe a shot of Cole's whiskey."

"You know about that?"

She nodded, one side of her buttery mouth slightly upturned. "Cole's all-purpose medicine."

"You make it sound like I'm an alcoholic." Cole, who had somehow materialized, was leaning in between us.

"It helped me once or thrice," Amy said, a wistful smile on her face. "I wouldn't refuse any."

I wondered about that for a moment and then remembered that she and Owen had found out about the cancer a week or so before they left for camp.

"How about you wipe your face first," I said, handing her a napkin.

"You two want to sneak off with me now, or shall we save it?" he asked conspiratorially.

Amy raised her eyebrows behind her napkin and looked at me. "Either way. Neil?"

I gulped. "I—I can wait."

After a pause, she nodded. "Okay." She looked up at Cole. "We'll wait 'til the bonfire."

"Okay." Cole grinned, tapping his front jeans pocket, and when my eyes followed the movement, I couldn't help but notice the not-inconsiderable mound in the crotch of his pants.

Holy shit! What did he have in there?

"You just let me know."

"Know?" I ripped my eyes away from his bulge.

Our eyes locked. His bored into mine. The twinkle had turned into a blaze. He'd caught me. There could be no doubt.

And damn if my cock didn't betray me once more as it shifted in my jeans.

His smile grew even broader and he winked. "About the whiskey, Big Daddy," he lied, glanced down at my crotch, and then turned and walked away.

THE CAMPFIRE was huge, almost comically so, as people tried to approach it with their marshmallows on sticks. The heat from the near inferno was intense. I got close, lit mine on fire, and quickly stepped away. No slow browning for me. The temperature was just too much on my tender—albeit only slightly burned—skin. Plus I'd always loved my marshmallows blackened on the outside and gooey hot on the inside.

"I can't believe you did that," Amy said as I mashed my burned mess between chocolate and graham crackers.

I shrugged. "They're perfect this way." I took a bite of my sticky treat. "Not too hot or too cold." It was wonderful, like everything else here. "You, on the other hand, are risking incineration from standing around that conflagration trying to perfectly brown yours." I pointed to the admittedly perfect marshmallow at the end of her stick. "I mean, you're just going to mash it in your s'more anyway."

She grinned, and we both started laughing.

"Kettle corn?"

It was Cole—with two bags overflowing with popcorn.

"Sure." Amy took one of the brightly colored, movie-style bags.

"Daddy?" Cole asked, his eyes dancing in the light from the fire.

"Thanks." I took the proffered bag. "Do you grow your own popcorn too?" I asked with a grin.

"Nope, but Cook does make the mixings to turn it sweet. You've got chocolate on your face."

Before I knew what he was doing, he reached out, wiped the corner of my mouth, and offered an upraised finger to me. Immediately, I felt a tightening in the crotch of my jeans as I looked from the chocolate on the tip of his big index finger to his eyes and back again. Those eyes were flashing again, and I could see the "I dare you" in them. My breath caught. Taking the choice away from me, he stuck his finger in his own mouth and sucked it clean.

Amy cleared her throat, and I jerked. We turned to her in unison. Both her brows were raised high enough that they'd disappeared under the hair that covered her forehead. "If you two are through, how about some of that whiskey, Cole? I could sure use a drink, and I think Neil here could too."

"You bet," Cole said. "But let's slip back a bit, out of the light where everyone can see us."

We did, which meant Amy couldn't see the daggers I'd shot her with my eyes.

"What the hell was that?" I murmured.

"I was thinking of asking you the same thing," she replied.

For one second, I thought I might either throw up or run away. Until I realized there was no reproach in her voice. None at all. My stomach began to flip.

Cole wiggled up close to us and grinned. "I feel like I'm at the high school prom sneaking booze into the punch."

"You spiked the punch," Amy said. She couldn't disguise the glee in her voice.

"I sure did."

"Me too," she whispered and burst into laughter.

"That was you?" I asked in shock.

"Yup," she said and took the flask from Cole. She took a drink and winced only slightly.

"Good Kentucky whiskey," Cole had said.

She gave a slight cough. "Of course, I used vodka to spike the punch. Not whiskey. Much easier to disguise."

That was the truth. The homecoming queen had almost fallen off the stage.

"I'm not so much worried about that tonight," he replied. "Guess I'm just into feeling a little naughty." Then he looked straight at me.

My breath caught, and Cole drank. I watched his throat move as the burning alcohol went down. That throat. Even that was sexy. Strong.

A man's throat.

Could a throat be sexy?

My pulse quickened. I felt sweat rolling down my ribs.

Then he handed me the flask. Our fingers not only touched this time, they intertwined. And dammit, I did nothing to stop it. My heart was pounding now. Our eyes locked.

He leaned in. "You're driving me crazy," he whispered, and I hoped Amy didn't hear. But how could she help it? She was barely two feet away. "You gotta make up your mind."

Make up my mind? What the fuck was that supposed to mean?

I pulled the whiskey away from him and took a long swig.

"Hold on there, partner," Amy drawled. "Save some for us, old hoss."

I started to cough, and Cole slapped my back and—*damn it, damn it, damn it!*—even that touch heated me up. When I stopped coughing, I choked out, "Damn!"

Cole was standing so close. I felt my cock moving, looking for room to stretch out. It was his eyes.

"I've got to go," I said and spun away.

"Neil," Amy called out.

"You okay, Big Daddy?" Cole's voice, even raised in worry, was like honey.

I got about two feet before Amy grabbed my arm. I pulled away.

"Neil? Babe?" I couldn't see her face. The flames were behind her, silhouetting her.

"You're driving me crazy," he'd whispered. *"You gotta make up your mind."*

No! No decision to be made. I couldn't go back. I'd escaped it all these years. I couldn't go back.

I started to tremble. I backed away.

"Neil?"

"Let him go," Cole said.

I turned and ran.

I had to get out of there, and I had to get away as fast as I could.

THAT NIGHT, I had a very intense dream.

I was soaking in the hot tub when I heard a noise. A sort of gurgling. Curious, I climbed naked from the water and went to the gate.

Me. Without a towel.

How did I not know it was a dream? How do we dream such things and not know it can't be real?

"Hello?" I asked.

Nothing.

I opened the gate, as casually as could be, worried not in the least about being naked.

There before me was a *huge* black bear.

I froze, terrified.

It reared up on its hind legs, looking like it must be ten feet tall. More. Fifteen feet. Who measured such things in the world of sleep?

The bear lunged forward, and of course I couldn't move. I screamed, and it threw its shaggy arms around me, its huge mouth open wide, and I could actually feel its hot breath, feel the claws on my back—so sharp. It was so real!

I tried to wake myself, finally knowing this couldn't be real. Hoping it wasn't. Begging that it wasn't. But in Morpheus's realm I stayed.

And then the great bear began to change.

It began to shift, its flesh moving and flowing. Like a candle, the bear began to melt, transforming against me. The hair was retreating into its body, disappearing, the snout shrinking away, its form growing smaller and slimmer, and then...

...and then it was Cole.

He was naked.

His arms were still wrapped around me, his hands on my shoulder blades, and he was looking at me, *into* me, with those exotic eyes.

Eyes filled with pure lust.

I felt his hardness against me, and when I looked—for some reason I *could* see—I saw he was fully erect, his cock throbbing with excitement.

He kissed me.

My heart felt like it would explode inside my chest.

He thrust his cock against mine and, oh yes, I was hard too! His skin was smooth, so smooth, and it was crushing up against the thick hair on my own chest. It felt so damned real and, even in the dream, I sensed the irony of how now *I* was the hairy one.

The kiss seemed to go on forever, and a heat rose up within me. Below, our cocks were dueling, slipping, sliding, crushing against each other....

Abruptly Cole pulled back.

I cried out from wanting his lips on mine. Then he fell to his knees and took my thick length into his mouth. It was so wet and warm and *real*!

When I looked down at that masculine, beautiful man sucking me, it was over. I came violently and awoke with a shout.

I discovered I had ejaculated all over myself. My chest and belly were covered in my seed. I hadn't had an orgasm with so much semen since I was a teen.

And when had I last had a wet dream? Years?

Fuck! I couldn't escape Cole. Not even when I slept. This had to stop or I was doomed.

CHAPTER 8
Dealing with It

THE NEXT morning at breakfast, I realized I needed to make a quick trip back to my cabin before the day's activities began. I'd made a little mistake. There had been a failure to communicate. Thankfully, I had the little golf cart, so it wouldn't take long to take care of it.

We were going on a hike that morning, and since it was supposed to be a hot day, I'd figured it might be a good idea to wear shorts.

Nope.

Cole strongly advised we all wear jeans for protection against the nettles and thistles.

And boots to protect us from snakes.

Snakes…! How had I forgotten about the snakes?

Western diamondbacks. Timber rattlers. Western pygmy rattlesnakes.

And copperheads. Copperheads were snakes that instead of slithering off when they heard people coming, or coiling up and shaking their rattles, elected to play dead. And if you stepped on them, they bit you!

I shuddered at the thought. Jeans and cowboy boots it was.

It didn't help that I wasn't having the best morning. Cole had been distant—could I blame him?—but professional. I felt a tension that all but ruined my mood of the last few days.

I was leaving the dining room to dash back to my cabin to change when I noticed Darla Clark was in her office.

I looked back into the dining room at Cole. My heart skipped in my chest. My stomach did that clench thing it had been doing a lot of since I'd gotten to Black Bear. I looked at Darla again.

And then I made a decision.

I walked to the door, stood there looking at her, building my courage, then glanced back into the main hall.

But it wasn't Cole I saw. It was the towering stuffed bear, its arm upraised.

That did it.

I knocked on the threshold of her office. She looked up and her expression turned from one of studious concentration to a very big smile. Her whole face brightened. "Good morning, Mr. Baxter!"

Would she still be smiling after I spoke with her?

"Neil," I said.

She nodded. "Neil."

I opened my mouth and dammit, the words just wouldn't come. What did I say? What was I asking? I didn't know how to start.

Cole is coming on to me, and I don't like gay men?

"Are you all right?" she asked, concern now filling her face.

"I… I don't know," I stammered. "I don't know where to start, how to…."

"Please, sit down," she said, then got up and gestured to the chair in front of her desk. I did as she said, and she closed her office door. She sat before me on the edge of her desk. She was wearing a classic cowgirl outfit in navy and pale blue, with matching boots and a bolo tie. I noticed a blue cowboy hat hanging from a peg on the wall. Not what I was used to seeing a woman her age—was she sixty-five, maybe?—wearing. And somehow, she did it all without looking ridiculous. Adorable might have been the right word.

It made my stomach relax a *little* bit.

But not much.

"What's this about? Is it your cabin?"

My cabin?

"I know it's a little out of the way, and I'm sure you would have preferred to be with your fam—"

"Oh! Oh no." My cabin was perfect. I took a deep breath. "Mrs. Clark. It—"

"Darla, please."

Damn! Why did she have to stop me? Was I going to get this out? I had to.

This wasn't a want. This was a need.

"It's about Cole," I said, anxiety sweeping over me. I felt my upper lip break out into a sweat.

"Cole?" she said, a gray eyebrow shooting up.

I nodded.

"Did Cole do something to upset you? Cole?"

I could see I'd stunned her. Was it possible she didn't know?

"Not *did* something exactly," I replied. Then, taking a deep breath: "Darla.... He's... he's gay!"

Darla nodded her head. "Yes, I know." She blinked at me. "What does that have to do with anything?"

"That's not enough?" I cried.

"Mr.—*Neil*." She paused. "I know Cole is gay."

"You *do*?" I asked.

"Of course," she replied. "And I can't see how it could possibly be a problem." Any sympathy had disappeared from her expression. "Unless he's behaved improperly, that is—and mind you, I find that very hard to believe."

"I... I...." What was happening to the world? How could she be so casual?

Amy was okay with Cole being gay. Her kids were. My own daughter.

And now an older woman as well? Didn't country women have a different moral standard than city people? I always thought gay men had a hard time of it in small towns. I figured a ranch would be the same. It was one thing for gay men to hang out in their inner-city gay ghettos. It was one thing for them to make merry in decadent places like San Francisco or Key West or Provincetown. But Black Bear Ranch? Where people brought their families?

Would Darla be so casual if she knew that Cole had made sexual advances to me? At least twice? Would that be okay too?

Yet now, with Darla's attitude—with that almost steely expression on her face—I found myself unable to tell her.

"I can't be the first to be concerned about his... lifestyle," I said, finally finding my voice. "Your guests.... I've chatted with some of them. A lot of them are country folk. There's a truck driver. A pastor. A preschool teacher. And that's not even counting the families with children. Little kids! I can't believe no one else has said anything."

Her brows came together, a dark cloud seeming to form over her head.

Not good.

"First, *Neil*, what Cole does in private is none of my business, and frankly none of yours either."

It certainly was if Cole was hitting on me! But before I could say that, she continued.

"Neil. It's also the twenty-first century. Same-sex marriage is legal now. Intolerance of other people's lifestyles or choices or orientations—that's becoming a thing of the past."

Damn. It was almost exactly what Crystal had said.

"Second, I don't match Cole up with people uncomfortable with homosexuality. Or with rednecks and church groups—especially conservative church groups. And we get 'em! I'm not stupid. I match him up with gay groups or open-minded individuals." There was no missing her emphasis on the word "open-minded." She leaned back on her desk. "He doesn't advertise his sexuality, but he isn't hiding either. Your family knows about him. They have for years. And so he's open with them."

I sat there, stunned, looking up at her. My head was swirling. I didn't know what to say. She was right. My family did know. And loved him. And as far as the more conservative guests I had chatted with, well, none of them had even mentioned Cole's sexuality. They'd only talked about his friendliness or his singing or his riding ability. Either there were a lot more open-minded people than I had ever guessed, or it was like Darla said. He'd just kept that part of himself to himself.

But what about the fact that he'd come on to me at my cabin? Suggested that he might come by and keep me company? That he'd made me very uncomfortable pointing out my "hobbit feet"? That he'd played suck-finger with me last night?

That I had a sex dream about him, that he was stirring feelings in me I'd been successfully keeping at bay most of my life?

No. I certainly wasn't going to tell her that last.

"What would you like me to do, Neil?"

I stood up and then just froze—like the stuffed bear in the foyer. I don't know what I'd thought her reaction was going to be, but that was not it. I took a deep breath.

"Darla, he makes me uncomfortable. I've never…. I'm not used to…."

"Neil," she said, leaning forward again, resting her palms on the edge of the desk. "I'm sorry to hear that. I can talk to him. The last thing I want you to be is uncomfortable. That's the opposite of what we pride ourselves on here at Black Bear." She paused. "But frankly, I'm surprised. Cole has been with us nearly eight years now, and we've never had a complaint. Sure, I've heard a few hateful comments when someone didn't know I heard them. Faggot. That kind of thing." She said this last with a distasteful look on her face. "Running a place like this, we're going to get rednecks. We're very popular with the church crowd, who come here to not only ride horses, but to have prayer retreats."

I nodded.

"But understand this. Vincent and I love Cole very much. He's family."

Shit, I thought. Her eyes had gone... not steely exactly... determined. There wasn't going to be much sympathy here.

"He's a good man, Neil. And a very good wrangler. He's a favorite with all the guests. He's almost always requested ahead of time."

Requested ahead of time? Had Amy requested Cole?

Wait. What had Crystal said? *I sure hope we get Cole again.*

"Surely you know your family loves Cole?"

Apparently....

"And, well, from what I've been observing, I thought you liked him too."

I sighed. Surprised myself when I trembled.

I had liked Cole. I did like Cole. Frankly, a little too much.

A lot too much.

"This is your third day. All the guests have become acquainted with their wranglers now. You can see the disruption it would cause if I were to switch Cole with someone else, can't you? Have you talked to your family about this? I bet it would make them unhappy. I could switch *you* into another group, but surely you don't want that."

Shit. No, no. I didn't want that.

"Look, I know this is your vacation and you want to enjoy yourself. We've already started off on the wrong foot by putting you in a cabin all by yourself, away from your family. So I'm guessing you don't want to be separated from them during the day."

"No. No, I don't," I muttered aloud.

"I don't know what to say about your feelings about homosexuality, except it really has no bearing here. Cole's private life has no bearing here."

What about the fact he's making passes at me? I wanted to shout. But the words stuck in my throat. I felt embarrassed. She was so sure Cole was strictly professional. Would she believe some of the things that had happened between us? Hell! Would she wonder if I'd led Cole on? Had I? With all the staring, had I done something to make him think I was interested? Shit! What about if what happened in the hot tub came to light? Fuck!

Suddenly, the walls seemed to be very close.

Claustrophobically close.

I needed to get out. Get outside. Where I could breathe. "I... I... I'm sorry!" I stepped back, almost tripping back into my chair.

"Are you all right, Mr. Baxter?"

"Neil," I said, and fled.

Outside was better. I didn't feel closed in. How could I with that gorgeous, open blue sky? I could breathe again—that air that smelled of growing things. I took it deep into my lungs. I sat down on the edge of the porch and just breathed. In. Out. In. *Slowly* out. My heart was racing, but after a moment, breathing that clear, magical air, I started to feel a little better.

"Neil?"

I looked up to see Darla Clark standing over me. "Tea?" she asked and handed me a large glass. I took it, the ice cubes tinkling like the chimes lining the porch, the sun shining off them like crystals. I took a long drink. Sweet.

Exactly as I liked it. Not too sweet. Perfect.

"Better?" she asked.

I managed a nod.

She sat down next to me.

"Is it a religious thing?"

I looked at her confused. "Religious thing?"

"Your problem with Cole. All that 'Thou shalt not lie with a man, as with woman—it is abomination' stuff."

I shook my head. "No." I looked back at the sky. There was a single cloud. And flying overhead that hawk or whatever it was. Floating on the air. Free. "I don't believe in God," I said.

Not my mother's God.

"I've always thought that was a load of bullshit," she said and swung her legs.

Had Darla Clark just said "bullshit"?

She went on. "What is it, then? If you don't believe in God, why do you care if someone's gay? It's usually the Bible quoters who have the problem."

"I'm just not used to it," I said.

"You've never known a gay man before?"

I didn't answer. I'd known gay men all right. Like the supervisor who showed me how gay men really were and treated me like I was a piece of meat. It seemed that any gay men I met only wanted to be sexual with me. And of course there was George. And just his name brought a twinge of the old guilt.

And Jack.

That made me tremble again.

And that wasn't mentioning... other things.

"They're not all sex fiends, you know," Darla said as if reading my mind. "They aren't trying to recruit you. Cole knows you were married."

Did he? Well, he knew I had a daughter. So why the passes?

"I shouldn't be telling you this, but Cole is in a bad place right now. He had a relationship end in a very, very bad way. Two years now and I haven't seen him go on a single date. The man really hurt Cole."

The man....

Wait....

Hurt Cole?

I looked over at Darla.

"A real damned bastard, but Cole loved him. Loved him with all of his heart. I think he was hearing wedding bells. And now...." She shook her head. "Now all I can do is hope he'll love someone again someday." She sighed. "He pretends, but I can tell that he's lonely. But I still don't think he's even close to ready."

And once more, I didn't know what to say. I'd gone into her office to tell her... I don't know what. That I thought it was inappropriate for a gay man to work a family ranch? That I was uncomfortable around him?

That I was scared to death of him and all he meant?

And now I was hearing how some bastard had hurt Cole? Deeply? And that she wasn't sure if he'd find love again? That he was lonely?

I understood that feeling.

"Give Cole a chance," she said.

Give him a chance? I thought, and then I remembered his dream kiss, a tingle spreading out over my arms. Damn!

"Neil, I believe we all come together in life for a reason, like Cole coming to live here."

Cole lived at Black Bear?

"Your family vacationing here for years. Now you. Who knows what's in the wind?"

I looked at her, truly looked at her…. Did she truly believe what she said? That we come together for a reason? Wasn't it all coincidence? That's what I had always believed. Or at least for a long, long time. What she was saying was akin to religion. And there was no place for religion in my life. But as I looked at Darla Clark, listened to her words, I couldn't help but wonder if this old cowgirl wasn't some kind of wise woman. Strange. Yet something felt immediately right in her words. It was like the air in my lungs.

"Okay," I said.

Darla laid a hand on my shoulder, and we sat there awhile and looked into the morning sunshine.

WE WOUND up starting our hike by walking to my cabin so I could change. Which of course meant I'd have to go back to the main building for my cart later. But hell, it wasn't that far.

My family was quite impressed with where I was staying, and Amy looked longingly at the hot tub.

"You can come over and use it any time," I said.

I changed clothes quickly, and then Cole led us to places we somehow hadn't seen before. Black Bear was huge, and it was gorgeous. We started following the creek behind my cabin and wound up walking through the woods where the water joined a small river. On the other side, we could see a large open field through the trees. Like everything, it was lovely. But to get to it we had to cross a rope-and-board bridge, which swayed as we walked over it. Luckily, it wasn't high at all, and the water looked shallow.

A moment later, we stood in front of a field ablaze with butterflies.

"Whoa" was all I could say. A large yellow-and-black-striped butterfly drifted by me before landing on a large purple thistle. It looked as big as my hand with its wings spread out.

Stunning.

"It's a tiger swallowtail," Cole said.

He even knows the names of the butterflies.

"And that," he said, pointing to a large black one with blue lower wings, "is a female. Some species you can't tell the males from the females."

"So the yellow one is male?" I asked.

"Maybe. The males are always yellow, but the females can be either black-and-blue *or* yellow."

"What about this one?" Crystal asked, and Cole moved off, presumably to identify it.

"How are you today, Neil?" Amy asked, walking up to me.

"Okay," I replied.

"You worried me the way you ran off last night, babe."

I turned to see her studying me with wide eyes. "I'm sorry."

"It's Cole, isn't it?"

My throat closed up.

"What's happening between you two?" she asked.

I started to protest and then saw there was no recrimination in those eyes.

"I don't know," I said, my voice cracking.

Amy slipped her hand into mine and squeezed. She didn't say anything for a while. We just walked, holding hands like two kids.

"At least your burn is gone," she finally said.

"It is?" I touched my face with my free hand.

"Did you use some of Cole's magic burn cream?"

I shook my head. "No."

"You're one lucky man," she said. "My family burns *so* easily, and *you* wake up the next day tan."

"What can I say?"

"It is a good thing you got the hat, though. It helped protect you from burning more. Even you'd have had trouble with a burn on top of a burn."

I nodded. Reached up and felt the hat. For some reason, it made me smile.

"It does look good on you," she replied.

My smile turned into a grin.

"I love you, Neil."

My stomach leapt. Love?

"I love you too, Amy. You're my best friend."

"Always," she said.

"Still missing Owen?" I asked.

"Oh, yes. Constantly. *Always.* I always will. Mom told me that. She said it would get better, though." She turned to me. "Does it?"

"It helps to have a best friend."

She managed a smile, and we walked off into the morning.

AFTER LUNCH, a marksmanship tournament was scheduled. I'd never been to such a thing. During a contest for some of the more seasoned guests, there were lessons for those of us who didn't know which end of the gun to point away from us—namely, me.

Cole was my teacher, of course.

He stood very close to me, showing me how to hold the rifle, practically putting his chin on my shoulder as he showed me how to line up the sight with my target. We were pretty much spooned together, and my face grew hot, both by his nearness and wondering what people were thinking.

"Now," he whispered, "when you think you have it, slowly, slowly let your finger pull the trigger."

He was using that honey voice again. He said it like sex. Like it wasn't a gun in my hands, like my finger wasn't on a trigger, but something else entirely.

My cock shifted in my jeans once more—damn the effect he had on me—and when I pulled that trigger I missed my target completely. Leaves in a tree high above the green bottle burst in the air.

Cole chuckled softly in my ear, but it didn't hurt my feelings. I could tell he wasn't laughing at me.

"First time, I hit my uncle's car," Cole said. "He was not amused."

And then he repeated his careful instructions.

I so wanted to hit that damned bottle. So wanted to impress him. *Please him?*

I did what he said. Lined that little piece of metal up with the V at the end of the rifle and the bottle and hoped, hoped, hoped—

"Don't close your eyes when you fire," he whispered and damn, if I hadn't been about to do that. Had done it the first time.

"It's okay," he said, voice as soft as Mystic's face. "Take a deep breath."

I did.

"Hold it...."

I did.

"Line 'er up."

Here goes nothing, I thought, and did as he said.

"And fire as soon as you're—"

I pulled the trigger.

An instant later the bottle exploded in a shower of green glass.

I grinned foolishly. I'd done it. I couldn't believe it! I'd hit that damned bottle.

Then in quick succession:

"You did it!" shouted my daughter.

Amy cheered.

And Cole hugged me hard from behind, his hands resting for one breath on my chest.

My legs almost went out from under me.

Cole held me only long enough so I didn't fall and then stood back. I shivered, despite the heat of the day. And even with the sun beating down hotly upon me, I could still feel *his* heat.

I shivered again.

"I knew you could do it," Cole said, smiling, those almond eyes even narrower than usual. For one frozen moment in time I thought he was going to kiss me. I almost leaned in to let him.

Then I felt a slap on my shoulder, and I turned to see Crystal give a little leap. "That was awesome, Dad! We'll turn you into a cowboy yet."

We practiced a little bit after that. I even got a few more bottles.

But then it was time for the entertainment, and that consisted of some stunningly impressive demonstrations from some of the wranglers.

The riding corral was decorated in bright colors—banners and flags and long, wide ribbons. There were even a bunch of mannequins dressed up like jesters and clowns—close to a dozen of them—wired to the fence posts around the corral. Each held a colored, helium-filled Mylar balloon.

But we were all taken aback when Vincent, the man who said so little, did all kinds of tricks, including shooting clay pigeons fired in the air, and more impressively, wooden blocks thrown into the air by the guests.

And, of course, there was Cole.

Why was I surprised?

He shot a row of bottles and cans along a fence top with precision, not missing one, and doing it faster than I'd been able to aim and fire just once—*bam! bam! bam! bambambambam!*—and then snatched up a second rifle and blew the top rail off the fence post with two shots, then shattered the opposite end, and still had two rounds left. We knew that because he fired them into the air.

Then, finally, it was Darla who took us all by surprise. Just when we thought the show was over, she came riding in on the back of her horse, firing at Mylar balloons. She didn't miss once.

I don't think I was the only one who was stunned.

"What?" she called out to the crowd. "You think I was born an old lady?"

And the crowd went wild!

Afterward was free time. Some people went hiking, some riding, and some of the guests went off for spa treatments. I'd forgotten to make an appointment, but hey, I had my own hot tub and was quickly becoming addicted to it. I knew where I was going.

Amy and I wound up walking Darla back. Cole had taken her horse to the stables because she had work to do at the office.

"That was amazing," I told her.

"Thank you."

"I never get tired of it," Amy told her. "I think you've gotta be the best shot on the ranch. Vincent and Cole are fantastic. But you—you should excuse the expression—blow them away."

Darla got a good laugh at that.

"It's my one real chance each week to do what I love. Ride and shoot." She sighed. "I miss my wranglin' days. I'm just not an office manager kind of girl, you know? But it's me or nobody. People just don't seem to understand Black Bear. I'm the only one who knows she is more than facts and figures in a ledger. More than rules and regulations. Black Bear is a lady...."

We'd reached the main hall by then, and Darla gave us a little shrug and a hopeless little half smile. "Well, daylight's a-wasting. Too bad I can't see it inside."

"Sorry, Darla."

Then she gave us a real Darla Clark smile, told us not to listen to the ramblings of an old lady, and headed inside.

"Kind of sad, isn't it?" Amy asked. "To have all this...." She swept her arm up and around us. "To love this land like she does. And to be cooped up inside all the time."

I didn't know what to say. I was just finally figuring out for myself that "outside"—even with its heat and dust and bugs and maybe snakes—wasn't something to be shunned.

I stretched and popped my back and told Amy that I was heading for my hot tub. "Join me?" I asked.

She immediately agreed.

It became one of the biggest turning points of my life.

WE TOOK the golf cart back to my cabin, and I didn't even think about the fact we hadn't stopped at hers.

It wasn't until we'd gone out back to my little fenced-in backyard, after I'd snagged my ludicrous trunks, that I suddenly realized Amy didn't have her swimsuit.

"Shit," I said. "Well, we can zip back in just a minute and—"

"Just turn your back, why don't you?"

I froze as she began to unbutton her blouse.

Was she…?

She pulled off her top and stood before me in her bra.

"You gonna turn around?" she asked, reaching back to undo the hooks. "You don't have to."

Holy shit! I thought and quickly turned on my cowboy-booted heel.

"I'm assuming you have towels?" she asked, and telling her I did, I dashed into the cabin for two of the big ones.

When I came back, she was standing in the tub, her back to me.

She hadn't settled down yet, and I could see half of her bottom. It was the first time I'd seen a naked woman in a long time. She looked like a Greek statue. Graceful. But….

Once again, that was all it was. As much as I had wished otherwise for my whole life, all Amy's bare body was to me was the beauty of some statue of Aphrodite or Artemis or Athena….

Lovely, like a deer or a horse or a tiger swallowtail.

But she did nothing sexual for me at all.

Was she trying to seduce me?

This could go bad fast.

She sat down with a long sigh and shifted so she was facing me. I could only see the tops of her breasts, thank goodness. Then she covered her eyes. "Your turn," she said.

Shit, shit, shit.

What was I going to do?

"You can do it," Amy said, sensing my nervousness even though her eyes were still closed. "I won't look. Promise."

I kicked off my boots, started to undo my own shirt, and realized I'd better hurry. I scrambled out of my clothes and, for the second time, stood naked to the world. This time I was not alone. I was so anxious I think my penis partially retreated into my body.

Do it! I thought, and I quickly climbed into the hot water. It was a small tub and our legs couldn't help but touch. *Damn. Damn, shit, and damn.* What was she up to? What if…?

She laid her head back. "This is so nice."

"Yes," I mumbled.

"Thanks. I needed this."

"You're welcome."

"And you're uncomfortable," she said without looking at me. "Don't be. We're friends, right?"

I nodded, then remembering she wasn't looking, said, "Yes."

"Yes to you're uncomfortable or yes to we're friends?" she asked.

I laughed. "Both, I guess."

She sat up, her breasts rising higher. I saw a flash of areola through the bubbles. "Neil," she said.

Crap! What was she about to ask?

"This thing between you and Cole…."

"Cole?" I said, voice cracking. Now that was not what I was expecting. Ugh. Why was she asking about him?

"Do you like him?"

My brain locked up. *Like him?* My heart began to race. What was she getting at? Did she know? She couldn't know.

Why couldn't she? She has eyes.

Amy sighed. "Oh, my sweet, dear, lovely bestest of friends."

I literally felt like I might explode.

She leaned forward, pushing her breasts beneath the churning water, and reached out and stroked my temple. "What's going on in here?"

"I… I…. What do you mean?" I don't know how I even got those words out.

"What is it about you and the whole gay thing?"

"What do you mean?" My mouth was so dry I could hardly talk.

"So uncomfortable. I remember you quit a job because you had a gay supervisor. It always confused Em and me."

The gay supervisor. The one who had basically let me know that he was looking to promote someone. That he was trying to decide between two people. Me and one other guy. And he told me that while he was standing next to me at the urinals. He told me and he stared at my penis. He stepped back and showed me his.

Yes.

I had quit.

"You two talked about that?" I said, amazed.

And disturbed.

"Of course we did. She wondered why you quit just because you had a gay boss."

I shook. "It wasn't 'just' because he was gay." And then I told her. Told her all about it. And how for a moment—one that seemed eternal—the man had actually tempted me.

"She'd wondered if you'd had an affair with him."

"What!" I cried.

"She thought maybe you'd been with him and then got to feeling guilty or something."

"She told you that?" I was stunned. Stunned that she thought I would cheat on her. Stunned that she'd told Amy.

"Yes," Amy said.

"Why?" Why would my wife and her sister talk about such things?

"Em wanted to talk to you about it. Had wanted to for a while after it happened, when you were settled in your new job. She'd made up her mind, actually. She was finally going to confront you. But then...."

There was no reason for Amy to finish her sentence. Emily had died.

The pain came back. The missing her came back.

I swallowed hard.

Amy looked deep into my eyes. "She knew, Neil."

"Knew what?" I squeaked out.

"That you're gay."

There was nothing Amy could have said that would have stunned me more. I jolted. My whole body went rigid. Sound amplified. The bubbles sounded like a churning flood. The chirping birds echoed in my head. I quite suddenly wanted to cry. The tears were filling my eyes. "Why... why would you think I'm...?" My mouth stopped working. I couldn't say the word. "Why would you think *that*?"

Amy leaned back and her breasts rose from the water, fully exposed.

Quickly, I looked away. "Amy!" She had completely shocked me. She was naked. Well, of course she was naked, but…. But she was my friend. My wife's sister. She was….

"Neil, it's okay."

"You're my wife's sister!" I protested aloud.

"That isn't it, though, is it? Any man would at least sneak a peek. My *brother* would. That's what men do. Hey, I've got a great rack!" She started to laugh.

"Amy," I muttered. I was horrified.

"Look at me," she said softly. There was… love in her voice.

Enough that I almost did look. But no! No, I couldn't.

"Neil, look. It's okay. They're just breasts."

I closed my eyes, a million years passed, and then I looked.

Amy's breasts. I stared. They were bigger than Em's. I supposed they were beautiful. Supposed she was right. Any man would have wanted to look. She was a beautiful woman. But, once again. Nothing. *Nothing.* Why did they do absolutely nothing for me?

"Nothing. Right?"

"You're beautiful," I said. But like a deer or a horse or a tiger swallowtail.

A tear slipped down my face. I shook my head.

Amy settled, allowing the bubbles to cover her again, and I felt a slight relief.

"You're gay," Amy said.

"No," I whispered.

"Neil?"

I looked into her lovely eyes. Looked for the judgment. The recrimination. The disgust. There was nothing but love there. *And why would there be anything else?* I asked myself. Hadn't she said it didn't bother her that Cole was gay? In fact, she'd gotten pretty mad at me the other day—something she almost never did—when I was upset about Cole's gayness. Hell, when had that been? A day ago? Two? A thousand years? She'd said she couldn't believe I was upset and told me that Cole was "a very nice young man."

But this was different! This was me, dammit, not some boy wrangler on a ranch in the middle of nowhere.

"You're gay, Neil," she said again, and I bristled at the idea.

I shook my head. No. Not gay. I could just appreciate the male form, that's all. Like that horse or that butterfly. But not…. Not….

"Em knew," Amy repeated. "It's okay."

I fell back, completely shocked. "*What*?"

"Em always knew. Way back. When you showed up at the house needing a place to stay. She knew something was up then."

The surreal moment became even more dreamlike. What the hell had happened? One minute I was walking through a field of flowers and looking at butterflies, and the next thing I knew I was naked in a hot tub with my sister-in-law asking if I was gay. No, telling me I was gay. She *knew* I was gay. It was like I was in an episode of *The Twilight Zone*.

"It was the night the police showed up."

I went numb.

That night.

"You showed up, and then Mom called the police, and that's when you came to stay with us for a while."

The numbness spread.

"Something about your mom, I never completely knew the story, which drove me crazy, because Em told me almost everything."

"She really didn't tell you?" I asked, surprised.

Amy shook her head. "Nope. But she did find out what happened with you and that track buddy of yours. He came around and said something to her after you and Em started to date seriously. He wasn't happy about it at all. He accused Em of stealing you."

Jack did what? "He said she stole me?"

Amy nodded. "He did, Neil."

I went from numb to light-headed. This was all too much. Jack had gone to Em about me? And no one had ever told me?

"He kept coming to me at school," I said. "He kept telling me he wanted to get together again. And all I could see was that girl jumping on him and licking his face, and it… it made me sick, Amy. I kept thinking that my mom was right. That gay sex made you evil."

"You really thought that?"

I looked at her and nodded.

Yes. I had really thought that.

Then Amy nodded. "I guess that explains it. He told her that the two of you had started something very special and she had ruined it."

I could only stare. "She knew that Jack and I…?"

She nodded again.

"All that time…." Em had always known I…? That I liked…? I thought I was going to faint.

The world wavered in and out; then Amy was next to me, arm around me, her left breast pressed against my chest. "Neil. Babe. It's okay."

"No. No, it's not!" The world was coming to an end.

"Yes, it is."

I shook my head. World—was—ending.

"Em thought he was lying at first, but then she started to notice little things."

Little things?

"The way you would look at some guy, the fact you never tried anything sexual with her, never tried to… you know… feel her up the way guys had tried to do with her before. That you wanted to wait until the two of you got married before you had sex…."

"Em talked to you about shit like this?" I gasped.

Amy nodded. "Of course she did. We were sisters. You were an only child, so you probably don't know about things like that. But sisters talk. We talk about boys. We talk about men. We talk about sex. Or we did. Emily and I were a lot closer than most sisters."

Somewhere along the line, I had started crying, although I didn't know when.

"Em thought I was gay?"

"It's okay. She didn't mind. You made love to her. Not often, but…."

Again, I thought I might faint. They talked about our sex life? *I* didn't *think* about our sex life! They *talked* about it?

"It wasn't that important to Em. She didn't really care that you two didn't make love very often. She liked sex, but she wasn't the little horndog I am." Amy laughed.

"This isn't happening," I whispered.

"Yes, it is. And I think it's way, way past time it did. Em decided to talk to you and changed her mind a thousand times through the years. She wondered why you were with her."

"I *loved* her," I all but shouted.

Amy nodded. "Yes, I believe you did. So did Emily. But she could tell you weren't fulfilled by her."

"Of course I was," I protested. "She was all I had. All there was. She was my compass. The only damned reason my life had any direction. You saw! You saw I nearly died with her."

"She worried one day you'd finally leave her."

The tears were pouring down my face now. "Why are you telling me this?"

Amy sighed and leaned back. "Because it's time you hear it. It's been too long coming."

I tried to look at her, but she was a blur. "What the hell are you talking about?"

She took a deep breath. "You know how you asked me why I wanted you to come with me for my vacation? You don't understand why I'd want to be here, right? Because I came here so many years with Owen."

I nodded. "You're right. I don't understand."

"I wanted to lose myself in Owen before he's gone."

Before he's gone? What was she talking about? Owen was buried—gone!

Maybe I was dreaming? None of this was making any sense. A bear would show up any moment.

And then I would wake up. Yes.

Wake up, I shouted in my head.

"Before all that's left of Owen is a memory. Before I need pictures to remember what he looked like." Now Amy was crying. "It's already hard to remember. I keep seeing how he looked in the hospital at the end instead of the sweet young man he was when we met, the smile he used to get me to go on those first dates. God, I loved him so much."

"Amy," I said, reaching out and touching her shoulder.

"I know he'll begin to fade, and before he does, I want to be around everything that reminds me of all the good times, so *that's* the way I remember him instead of that... dried up mummy." A sob escaped her.

My heart melted, and I started to cry again.

"Babe," Amy said, "*you* need to deal with your ghosts once and for all. And I don't mean Em. I mean whatever it was that fucked you up *before* Em."

"What do you mean?" I sighed.

"Have you ever made love with a man?" Amy asked.

"No!" This time I did shout.

"But you've been with men?"

"No! I… yes… no."

"Which is it, Neil?"

I almost took off once again, but before I could, she reached out and took my wrist in her hand. "No. Don't you *dare* run away again. You've been running all your life. You've gotta stop running sometime."

I looked at her, and the tears got thick again, and she went out of focus.

"Tell me, Neil."

"I… I can't" was all I could say.

She sighed again. "All right." She dropped her head back, and neither of us spoke for a long time. Then she said, "Look. Is that a hawk?"

I looked up and couldn't see anything, so I wiped my eyes, then looked again. It was the lone bird I'd seen, what, twice now? Was that yesterday? The day before?

"It looks lonely, don't you think?" Amy asked.

"Free," I said. "I think it looks free."

Neither of us spoke for a moment.

"Don't you want to be free?" Amy said.

The world blurred out again, and Amy took me in her arms. This time our nudity didn't bother me. We were just people, after all. Different body parts, but people. And it felt good to be held. I cried some more.

Then a thought began to rise. It rose with a shocking and crystal clarity I could not deny.

Just body parts? It feels good to be held?

Was that the reasoning that had allowed me to get involved with Emily in the first place? *Just body parts?* Did I convince myself it didn't matter what kind of body she had? That love was love? Had I cast aside a lifetime of being held by a man by deluding myself that being held by someone who loved me was all that mattered?

I pulled back. "Oh damn, Amy."

And I began to talk.

Finally.

CHAPTER 9
Retrospect

BUT FIRST we dressed and went into my cabin. I made coffee, not giving a shit that I wouldn't be able to sleep. Hell, there was always the whiskey.

We sat on the front porch, and I remembered the morning with Cole.... Was that today? Yesterday? Yesterday, yes.

I asked Amy if she thought I had hobbit feet, and she laughed until she choked.

"I've always thought so," she said. "Even before the movies."

Somewhere around then we left behind carefree banter, and I began to talk.

I was eighteen before I truly realized I was attracted to men and the incident with George at church camp, the incidents, hadn't just been some kind of experiment. Looking back, I don't know how I couldn't have known. All I had to do was see a man take off his shirt on TV and my attention was riveted to the screen. Locker rooms were both a nightmare and the fuel for wet dreams. Photographs of a nude South American man or an Aboriginal in *National Geographic* held far more promise or excitement to me than a *Penthouse* magazine, unless there was a special spread showing a woman and a man together. A glimpse of cock was all I needed and I was excited and masturbating, and like most red-blooded teenage boys, I masturbated a lot. How could I have not *known* I liked men? How had I convinced myself otherwise? How did I delude myself into believing that I liked women? I don't know.

I suppose it was fear.

No. No supposing about it.

It was fear.

Attracted to men.

I was attracted to men.

And damn! There was that school counselor. The one who told me that it was perfectly normal for boys to fool around with boys. "Experimenting" was the word he used. Funny how I so suddenly remembered that. *Experimenting.*

"What was it exactly you two did?" he had asked me, sitting so close to me our thighs touched. And that hand on my shoulder.

Mr. Morcant. His name came to me then, hard and fast, and I felt nauseous. Like I might puke.

He'd gotten me to tell him all about what George and I did—had pressed for details. He'd told me that what the two of us had done was perfectly normal. He'd told me all about my raging hormones and that boys my age couldn't—*shouldn't*—fool around with girls. He told me *that* would be wrong, and that I could get a girl pregnant—and that there was nothing wrong with us "helping each other out."

"In fact," he'd said, "it's beautiful."

And then he'd laid his hand on my leg and I saw the front of his dress slacks were all bulged out, and I knew just what that meant.

He was hard.

Mr. Morcant was excited.

Somehow I got out of there. Was it a phone call? His intercom?

I never went back. He'd only proved to me what I'd read in *Everything You Always Wanted to Know About Sex (But Were Afraid to Ask)*. That homosexuals were depraved. That all they did was search and search and search for the perfect penis—that's why they were so promiscuous—and that they would never *ever* find the perfect penis because the perfect penis was their *own* penis and what they needed was a vagina.

"My God," Amy said. "This happened when you were in junior high school?"

I nodded.

"Thank God you got away from him."

As if God had anything to do with it one way or the other, I thought, fighting back a sneer. I didn't want her to think I meant it for her.

After that day in Mr. Morcant's office, I held desperately to the thought and hope that one day I would get married and would want her vagina, and I'd want to be sexual with a woman and I would think that beautiful.

But that didn't happen.

As much as I loved Emily, as much as she was truly my compass, always pointing me north, I never felt for her what I had felt for George. Or Jack.

I was, *am*, a white male, and decent looking. The world should've been my oyster.

But I was different.

And dammit, I didn't want to be different!

So I tried to forget things. Pretend they didn't exist. That they never happened.

Like those issues of *National Geographic*.

Those issues of *Penthouse*.

Dirk Benedict.

I was only a kid when I saw this movie called *Sssssss* one night late on television when I thought my mother had gone to bed. There was this scene... I wish I could explain it. Terrible movie, I realize now, but for a kid, it was awesome. Young man gets turned into a giant snake by an evil scientist. What's not for a boy to love?

The thing is, there was this scene where the hero, played by Dirk Benedict, was going skinny-dipping with this girl. And she had these thick glasses. The two undressed, and as he dropped his pants, she took off her glasses, and the movie went out of focus. I remembered crying out, hurt by it.

Then to my horror, I saw my mother standing there. She'd happened to be going through the room when it happened. We stared at each other for... forever. She turned off the TV. I was so upset. I didn't understand what was going on inside me, but Mother did. She got down on her knees and made me pray for forgiveness. I didn't even understand what I was asking forgiveness for.

Amy had been holding my hand through this part of the story and she was doing what she did best. Listening. Barely said a word. Not that she couldn't talk the leg off a chair. But right then listening was what she was doing.

She stopped me only so she could go refill her mug.

Amy, who could easily drink a pot of coffee a day. Sometimes two.

WHEN SHE got back, I told her what had happened a year later when I was in fourth grade.

My friend Rod and I—"That really was his name," I told her—snuck into an R-rated action flick at the local theater when we were supposed to be seeing a Disney movie (the only thing Mom would let me see). There was a scene where the hero somehow wound up tied down in his underwear and tortured. I don't remember which actor he was or even the name of the movie. All I know is I couldn't stop staring at his bare chest and the mound in the front of his underwear.

As it turned out, Rod was spending the night at my house, and we decided to reenact the scene. It turned out Rod liked it as much as I did. First, Rod played the hero, and I tied him to my twin bed with a jump rope and an extension cord. Like the hero, all he was wearing was his Fruit of the Looms, and I couldn't keep my eyes off the small bulge in those undies. I wanted to touch him there, and I was so excited, but I didn't know why.

Then it was my turn to get tied to the bed. Rod didn't bother to get dressed. We were both hard as could be, tenting out the front of our underwear, when my mother—without knocking—walked into the room.

There was this frozen moment, and then she sort of went insane. She started screaming about sin and hell, and she was hitting me with this belt, and I couldn't move. I was still tied to the bed. The buckle… she hit me with the buckle end. Rod ran for home. Not long after, there were police. They took me away for a while—the childhood memory isn't clear. Was it a few days? A few weeks?

I sort of blotted it all out after I was allowed to go home. I never saw Rod again, and pictures of Jesus replaced the posters of Tarzan and Superman in my room.

How did I not know I was attracted to my own sex?

How did I *not* know?

IT WAS my turn for coffee then, and Amy used the opportunity to go ahead and top hers off. After I went to the bathroom to relieve myself. Coffee went right through me.

Then we settled at the kitchen table.

It was closer to the coffee.

Amy urged me to continue. She knew my story was far from over.

Years after my night with Rod, on my eighteenth birthday, my friend Jack, who I'd gotten buddy-buddy with in track, decided to make my birthday one I'd never forget.

He was right. It was a birthday I would never forget.

I wanted to be around Jack whenever I could. I always looked at him in the shower after track—his smooth chest, his round ass, his long penis—and here was another example! How did I *not* know I was attracted to my own sex? At first, Mom was okay with Jack. He was very masculine, and his parents were cornerstones of the church she went to at the time. She said he was the sort of influence I needed.

What do they say about preacher's daughters? Jack wasn't the daughter of a preacher, but the principle was the same. Jack was a sex fiend. If he wasn't lying, he'd lost his virginity at twelve. And he loved to tell me the stories. In detail. Stories that gave me all kinds of fuel for my late-night masturbation. But in my imaginings, there were no girls around. Just me and Jack.

Jack couldn't stand that I was a virgin, and he decided to take care of it. He got us double dates with a couple of girls who had reputations for being wild. Their reputations were valid. At their instigation, we got to playing this strange board game they'd gotten from Spencer's. To Jack's delight, it was a sex game. You moved your pieces around the board and rolled dice and had to do what these little cards told you to do.

One of those cards said that one of the girls (I can't remember her name) had to kiss the person sitting across from her. That turned out to be the other girl. To our surprise they laid a lip-lock on each other that made Jack howl with joy.

"Oh my fucking God!" he shouted.

Several drinks later, and halfway through the stack of cards, half our clothes were off—the game demanded that too—and I was both terrified and excited at the same time. My erection was plain, but that was okay. Both girls were in their underwear and one had just, without blinking her eyes, taken off her bra.

But then one of the girls drew a card where she could make any two people kiss. She chose me and Jack. When he told her there wasn't any way he was going to do that, she—I think it was his date—declared that was "No fair!"

"Wha' do you mean?" he slurred. The beers were kicking in.

"I kissed her," she whined, pointing to her friend.

"You want me to fucking kiss Neil?" He laughed.

"Uh-huh," she said, her voice dripping with sex, before she stunned us by dropping her hand to her crotch and rubbing herself through her panties. Above that, her breasts jiggled, and her nipples got hard right in front of us.

Jack looked at me, looked at her, looked at me again, and then looked at her hand. Before I knew what was going on, he'd leaned over the game, grabbed me by the back of my neck, and pulled me into a quick kiss. I was hardly aware it had happened, but my cock grew even harder, and I began to leak so heavily it left a wet spot on the front of my khaki shorts.

"Too fast," Jack's date protested. Donna. Her name was Donna.

Too fast, my mind echoed. *Way too fast!*

"Tough shit," he said and gave me a look I had no idea how to interpret.

There were no same-sex kisses for several rounds, and by then, both girls and I were in nothing but our underwear. Jack was the only one still in jeans.

"He's so hairy…," said Donna's friend—*my* "date." And I feel so bad that I cannot remember her name.

I blushed. How often had I thought about shaving my chest?

Jack looked at me and then down at himself.

"Is that a good thing or a bad thing?" he asked, and I nearly cringed waiting for her answer.

"A *good* thing," she all but panted.

Jack laughed and then looked at my chest—a little longer than I would have expected. It made things happen… down below, and I shivered. "I guess it's a good thing you're with *him*, then, huh?" He laughed again and told Donna to draw.

Donna read a card and somehow, suddenly, the girls were kissing like they were auditioning for a lesbian porn movie. Jack "whooped" through the whole show, and I could see the bulge in his jeans was straining to burst from its confines. He even had his own wet spot now—and that was through denim.

When the girls ended their kiss, Donna turned to him, eyes flashing. I could see the "I dare you" in those blue eyes. Her hand was working inside her panties, and Jack moaned in excitement.

"Kiss him," she gasped.

"Huh?" he said with a groan.

"Kiss him." And she was working that hand in earnest now. She brought it out and licked her fingers, and without a word, Jack spun on me, grabbed me, and this time the kiss was no quick peck. I struggled for only a second and then melted into him, my heart slamming inside my chest. When his mouth opened and his tongue demanded entry into mine, I let him in without hesitation. It was the most exciting thing that had ever happened to me in my life. My head was swimming, and I could taste the beer on his mouth and feel the stubble on his upper lip against mine like sandpaper, and it was exhilarating. I thought I would have an orgasm without touching myself. I heard moaning, and it was only when Jack finally pulled away I comprehended it was me.

Jack's eyes were dark, his pupils huge as he stared into mine. "I think Neil liked it," he said. He turned to our dates. "Don't you, girls?"

"Fuck, yeah!" said Donna. Her hands were still playing inside her panties. Her friend was rubbing herself as well.

"I think you liked it too," he told my date. Anne. It was Anne. Or Annie....

"Hell, yes," she exclaimed. "Gay sex is fucking hot!"

"How would you know?" he asked her as I sat there in a daze.

"We snuck one of her brother's gay magazines," Donna said, pointing to Anne/Annie, "and looked at the pictures of the dudes doin' it."

Jack's eyebrows shot up. "What's he got stuff like that for?"

"'Cause he's queer, you dumb shit!"

Jack's eyes darted back and forth between their crotches. "That works you two up, doesn't it?"

"Oh yes," Donna all but shouted. "We hid and watched her brother and his boyfriend fuck once. It was so damned hot. Got me so goddamned horny we fell out of the closet. Shocked them good! God, I wanted to jump in, but neither of them wanted me. I even offered my ass."

Jack's eyes grew huge. "Your ass? You'll take it in the ass?"

I couldn't believe the look on Jack's face—pure lust. Like he'd died and gone to heaven.

"I might," she said teasingly, drawing the two words out forever.

"What would I have to do to be able to tap me some of that?" he demanded.

"Suck his cock," she said without hesitation, pointing at me.

He laughed. "You want me to gobble my buddy's dick?" His voice was incredulous. He looked at me, and there was electricity sparkling, crackling in his eyes. His face was flushed.

"God yes," Donna said.

"You know neither of us is a fag, right?"

"That makes it even hotter," said Anne/Annie. "Straight men doing it? Oh. My. God!"

"What do you think about *that*, buddy?" He looked at me. "She wants me to suck your crank." Jack turned back to her. "I suck his cock and you'll let me fuck your butt?"

Donna grinned. "I want to taste his cum on your mouth when you kiss me," she said.

"You want me to take his cum?" he cried. "I ain't fuckin' doin' that!" Funny thing was, Jack looked anything but disgusted. He still looked pretty damned excited to me.

"Baby," she said, "you do that for me, and I'll do *anything* you want."

"Anything?" Jack said.

She grinned lasciviously. "Little pervert like you? I bet you got all kinds of nasty fantasies."

His eyes got even wider. I could see the wheels in his head spinning. "Will you lick my crack?" he asked. It was almost a gasp and a whisper at the same time. He was practically drooling.

Me? I couldn't move. It was like all this was happening to someone else.

Donna nodded vigorously. "Oh, yeah."

"You'd do that? Lick my asshole?"

"*No* problem! In a fucking heartbeat."

Jack moaned and, to my shock, he was on me like a pouncing animal. He shoved me back, ran his hands roughly through my chest hair—Anne moaned at that—and tore at the crotch of my underwear, letting my rigid erection spring into the open.

"Oh, yeah, *look* at that!" said one of the girls. "*So* hot!"

"Jesus, *dude*." Jack reached out and grabbed my cock. I thought I would have an orgasm on the spot. "This thing is huge," he said, and I looked down just in time to see him take me in his mouth.

I nearly screamed in pleasure. I'd never felt anything like it. Jack's mouth was so wet, hot, and tight, and he worked me like a calf sucking its mother's teat. The girls were urging him on, and that only seemed to inspire him. To my shock, Jack was moaning. He seemed to like what he was doing! In seconds, I was ready and tried to warn Jack, but I couldn't speak. Then I was unloading deep into his throat.

At first, I don't think he even knew what was happening. He'd nearly swallowed my cock, and I was shooting well past his taste buds. He must have figured it out, though, because he suddenly pulled back, and I finished shooting all over his face and my chest and belly.

"Fuck, man," he said and began to spit. Despite that he looked at me, his eyes flashing. "Wow, Neil. You could've warned me."

"I'm—I'm sorry."

Eyes still flashing, he began to wipe my cum from his face.

"No, don't," Donna yelled and she was on him faster than he'd pounced on me, licking at his face.

I fled.

I pulled on my clothes and was out the door faster than any race I'd ever run in track.

What happened next ensured I was never with another man again.

"What did happen?" Amy said.

"My mom tried to kill me," I whispered.

"What?"

I nodded, unable to say it again.

"Jesus," said Amy.

"Don't even fucking say *His* name," I barked.

Amy flinched at my words. "Wh-why?" She was rubbing my back. "Tell me, babe. What happened?"

I felt my eyes well up with tears again. *Damn.* I was some big fucking baby, wasn't I?

"Neil?"

I closed my eyes, fought back the tears, and wondered if I could answer her question. I had not told this story in twenty years. It was something I didn't like to think about, a memory I didn't like to recall; of course, the memory was always there.

I took a deep breath, let it out, took another. "I went home," I finally said. The hair on my arms was crawling as I continued. "I walked in the door, and she was fucking waiting for me. She'd pulled up a chair right in front of the door."

"Oh my God."

"Somehow she *knew*. She just knew. She stood up and did this sniffing thing. She said, 'I can smell it on you. Beer. And sex. And man. I can smell his *stuff* on you.'" I shuddered. "She knew."

"My Go—" Amy said and then stopped herself.

"Then she walked up to me and said, 'You can't shake it, can you? The demon named Homosexual. The demon that makes you want men.'

"I remember stepping back, telling her I was sorry and I'd do better, that I wanted Jesus to love me and I didn't want the demon. And you know what she said?"

Amy let out a sob. "Tell me, babe."

"She said it was too late. She said Jesus couldn't save me. That He didn't love me anymore. She said she was going to help me and told me it was better I was dead than live like that. And then she came at me with a knife."

"Neil! You can't be serious."

I nodded. I was serious all right.

"It's like something out of that movie *Carrie*," Amy cried. And she *was* crying. "Why didn't you ever tell?"

"I told Em. She told your parents. That's how I got to stay with you all."

The look of shock on Amy's face was priceless.

"So I guess Em didn't tell you everything?" I said.

"I guess not." She sagged like a puppet with its strings cut. "Jesus."

"I asked you not to say His name."

She looked back at me. "Why?"

"Because I rejected Him. He's supposed to be our savior, but He let *that* happen?" I shook my head. "No. Screw him! I gave Him up. Mom said He hated me and I was going to Hell. So why should I have anything to do with Him?" I shook my head again. "I don't know how I got out of there without her stabbing me, Amy. Adrenaline, I guess. Like you see in movies. Or read about where some mother lifts a car off her kid. Time slowed down. She was moving in slow motion, and I grabbed her and slammed her for all I was worth against the wall. And then I *ran*. And I left *Him* there with her."

"Oh, Neil." Amy shook her head. "I don't think He hates you."

"She disappeared," I said. "She moved away, and I never saw her again."

"Oh, Neil," she said again and laid her head on my shoulder. "I had no idea."

Neither of us said anything for a while, and then she said, "And Em knew about all of this?"

"Some of it."

"Oh, my friend." She sighed. "My dear, sweet friend. No wonder...."

"No wonder what?"

"You've made the choices you've made."

I pulled away. "What's wrong with my choices?" I asked, anger rising inside of me. "Could I have had a better companion than your sister?"

"N-no," Amy said.

"I miss her!" I cried. "Your mom says it gets easier? Well maybe. But not really. I miss her every fucking day. She was my *best* friend. I still forget. Something happens at work, and I want to call her and tell her. I see a movie preview on television and I think, Em would like that. A button comes off my shirt, and I realize she's not there to fix it, and I know it will take me an hour to do what she would have done in a minute. I miss her. And I don't regret the decision I made to be with her. *Ever.*"

"I didn't mean that, babe. I just meant...." She looked at me with those huge blue-green eyes.

"What did you mean?" I snapped.

"Oh, sweet Neil, if only—"

"If only what?" I shouted.

She flinched again, and a part of me felt shame.

"If only your mother hadn't been like she was. If she'd been accepting, your life would have been so different."

"Is that a *bad* thing?" I cried. "If I'd become some homo, I wouldn't have had Em. Or Crystal. Or *this* family. *You* wouldn't be in my life. Would you want that?"

Amy sighed. "And all those things are *good* things."

"So what, then?" I was almost crying once again, and I hated it.

There was a long silence again, and just as I thought Amy was never going to answer me, she said, "I wonder what it would have been like if the two of you had just been best friends...."

"Huh?" I asked her. What did that mean?

"Do you miss her friendship? Or do you miss her as a lover?"

The words stunned me.

I looked at her then, my soul aswirl with emotions.

And confusion.

"Wh-what's the difference?" I asked.

"There doesn't have to be," she replied. "But I wonder if it's time for you to have a lover. I wonder if it's time for the person who shares your bed to be everything that you need and not just a friend."

"What are you saying?" I asked, the confusion mounting. "That what Em and I had was a waste? That it wasn't good enough?"

She shook her head. "No. I think maybe it is exactly what you both needed. Like I said before. Em and I were very different. What *she* wanted more than anything in the world was friendship and companionship. She was never really into sex. Maybe a bit more than you, but she never regretted what the two of you had. And you?" She shrugged. "Like you said. If you hadn't gotten together there would be no Crystal. And no us."

She laid her hand on mine.

"But now? Now I think it's time for you to have more. And you aren't going to get that with a woman, Neil. You owe it to yourself."

I didn't know what to say.

"She wanted you to be happy, Neil. That was what she had made up her mind to tell you. That as long as she had your friendship, *she* was happy. She wanted you to have what she couldn't give you. She knew you needed to be with a man."

Stunned.

I was stunned.

"She loved you, Neil."

In a blink, I was crying again. *Damn it!* I *was* some big old fag, wasn't I?

She pulled me into her arms once more and… and it felt good.

It felt like how it had felt when I was very young and my mom would hold me, back before Pop left. Before she found Jesus big-time and filled the house with His pictures and made sure we went to church every Sunday morning and every Sunday night and every Wednesday night. Before she forced me to go to church camp and so many other things.

The moment with Amy was magic beyond magic. I was a little kid being held against a mother's breast. Safe. The way it was supposed to feel. Safe. Not scary. And not the tiniest bit erotic. Not one bit. And I told her so.

"Neil," she finally said, "I don't want to hurt you, but surely you know your mother was sick?"

I wanted to protest, but how could I? Of course Amy was right. My mother. She had been sick. Mentally unwell. And it took being held by a mother, by a real mother, to finally admit it to myself.

My mother was insane.

Instead of it hurting, like it had hurt for so long, the acknowledgment did something inside of me. The pain… lessened. Because the problem had been hers… not mine. Could it be that simple?

"Neil?"

And Amy's words.

She said I needed more than friendship. She said I needed to be with a man.

Was she right? Part of me wanted to fight it… but then I realized that part was my mother.

Because I did want more.

I did want a man.

I had tried to convince myself—for the most part I had—that friendship was all I had ever needed. That it didn't make any difference what package it came in, what kind of body, that love surpassed that.

But as I thought about Cole….

Dear God….

What he did to me with a simple look.

What had happened to me when it had been something as simple as our fingers touching as we passed a flask.

What had happened when he taught me to fire a rifle, and how just leaning into me had made me feel things I had never felt with Emily….

And I realized it was time to let her go.

What had Amy said?

"*Neil?*"

"Yes," I said after a long, long time.

And then something happened. I couldn't explain it. Something… lifted. It was like that phrase I'd heard a hundred times in my life. The one about a weight being lifted from your shoulders. I figured it was like saying "He laughed all the way to the bank." That it was just a saying.

But right then I felt it. I felt this… this weight… this very real weight… just lift away. Felt it in my shoulders.

The weight of my mother. Of my imagined failures. That I had failed Emily. The weight of fighting my… homosexuality. That I was…. That I was *gay*.

"Neil?"

I looked at her in amazement.

"It's time for you to let her go," she said.

"God, Amy," I said, feeling almost high. "I think I just did."

"Really?" she said, eyes wide and filled with hope.

I nodded. Then knew it. I had.

How? Why?

Was it the telling?

And yes, I realized. It was.

She squeezed me all the tighter. "Oh, Neil, I love you!" she said once again.

Tingling all over, I told her that I loved her too. Because I did.

"Neil?" she asked, while I floated like that hawk. "I think it's time for you to do something else."

"Something else?" I echoed.

"I think it's time you talk to Cole."

I pulled back. "Cole?"

She smiled. "The boy wants you. And I think you want him."

"*Amy!*" The old self-hatred threatened to rear up again. I could feel it too. And dammit, I couldn't allow that. If I did I would be lost forever. But the only way I could see that I could defeat it once and for all was to….

"Honey, if that boy wanted me, I'd go for him in an instant."

"I can't believe you're saying this." She might as well have told me to pursue a presidential campaign.

"Why not?" she asked me, her eyes dancing.

"Wouldn't I be betraying my whole life if I were to do that?"

"Why? You followed through. You were a good husband, and you've been an excellent father. You made promises and you kept them. Neil, Em is gone. *You* aren't. It's time, more than time, for *you* to live for you. Do it, by God!"

"By God?" I asked before I knew the words were even coming out of my mouth.

"Em would want it." Amy smiled. "Oh yes. She wanted you to be happy. *Be* happy, Neil. Haven't you been haunted by what you *thought* you should be long enough? Haven't you been possessed by your mother long enough?"

Yes! I had. The demon that was my mother's illness had possessed me. That was the demon, not me.

Because right then Cole's face came to my mind. His beautiful dark eyes. His smiling mouth. The trim, almost nonexistent goatee. The hair that looked so soft and begged to be touched. His arms, popping with muscles.

He was not a demon. He was the furthest thing from.

My heart started to pound. "You mean this, don't you?"

Amy's grin was huge, and she nodded with excitement. "Oh, yes."

I took a long, shuddering breath. This was too much to believe.

"You are attracted to Cole, aren't you?" Amy asked.

I looked at the Cole in my mind again—his smile, his flashing eyes, and felt a stirring in my loins. "Oh, Amy, you have no idea."

Sudden fear jolted through me. Could I do it?

"Tell him," Amy said.

Could it be that easy?

Easy?

Easy, hell!

What the fuck was I supposed to do? Walk up to him and say…. What? "Let's fuck?"

"Well, I hope you'd be a little classier than that," Amy said.

Damn! I blushed more fiercely. I'd said that out loud?

"Neil, you only get a few chances in life. You've waited long enough. Don't miss this opportunity."

"You think Cole could want me?"

Amy broke into laughter. "Oh Christ, Neil, I think so! I think so in a big way. *Ooops!* I said 'Christ,' didn't I?"

I laughed too. "Don't worry about it."

Amy sighed, reached out and touched my cheek again. "I don't know if you know this, but Cole was hurt pretty badly a few years ago. Every time we ask him if he's dating again, he tells us no. I was shocked to see him flirting with you. It was the last thing I was expecting."

There was that story again. Someone had hurt Cole. How could anyone hurt him? I found I was getting angry just thinking about it.

"I'll admit part of why I wanted you here at Black Bear was to meet him."

"What?" I said, my eyes going wide.

She nodded. "Not so you could bed him, mind you. I wanted you to have a positive role model. As sad as Cole has been, he's still so happy in himself. I wanted you to see gay men could be happy and normal. They're not all perverts, Neil. No more than any group of people. Men. Women. Gay. Straight. Lesbian. Bisexual. Whatever. That supervisor you once had. The way he treated you? It wasn't because he was gay. It was because he was an asshole. Men have treated women that way for years. Shit, for centuries."

"Yeah, maybe so. Mom would have said it was because *all* men are filled with the original sin of lust."

"Fuck what your mom thought," Amy said, and I looked at her agoggle. I wasn't sure if I had ever heard Amy say that word. "All gay men aren't like that supervisor."

I shuddered at the memory, but thoughts of Cole banished it.

"You aren't like that."

"You know," I said, "for a man who's not supposed to be a pervert, Cole sure has been coming on to me."

Amy laughed again. "I know. I can't believe it!"

I looked away, closed my eyes, let Cole fill my mind again. *Fuck!* Could I do this?

My heart started to pound again, and I looked back at Amy.

"You'd be a fool not to," she said.

"Amy." I sighed. "He's *so* young. He could be my son."

"Well, he *isn't*," she reminded me. "And what's age anyway? My mother is fifteen years younger than Pop."

"Cole's twenty years younger than me."

"So what? Besides, let's not get ahead of ourselves. Just because you two have the hots for each other doesn't mean wedding bells are chiming."

I hid my face in my hands. *Wedding bells?* I wanted to giggle. This was crazy!

How could things have changed so much in less than a week? It seemed impossible.

When I'd seen Cole's picture on the website, I'd been enthralled. I couldn't deny it. But then, when I realized he was gay, I was outraged to discover Black Bear Guest Ranch let him be a wrangler. Within seconds of meeting him, though, he'd begun to affect me.

And now?

During a short conversation in a hot tub, I'd let my mind go to schoolgirl fantasies of forever. "I'm acting like a teenager," I said through my fingers.

Amy took my hands in hers and pulled them down, looked at me, smiled. "Babe, in a way you are. You never pursued what was natural to you when you were young. I wouldn't be surprised if it's part of why you're attracted to Cole. It's your inner twentysomething dying to get out."

"You psychoanalyzing me, Amy?"

"Isn't that what I've been doing for the past hour? I'll bill you."

I shook my head. "Now you're being silly."

I looked away, and saw Cole's smiling face before me. Was I seriously considering this? Could I be sexual with a man after all these years of denying myself what I'd wanted? What if my mother's fucking ghost showed up right in the middle of things and I couldn't get it up?

"This isn't going to be easy."

"There's only one way to find out," Amy replied. "And you know what? I think Cole's the kind of man with the patience to help you work it out."

CHAPTER 10
Heroes

I DIDN'T know where to begin. How did I approach Cole? Was I truly considering doing this? I was a mess just thinking about it. What should I do? Should I say something? Get him flowers? Chocolates? I smiled. He'd liked that chocolate on my lips the other night.

Let things take their course, some inner voice told me.

That would be a lot easier, I thought with relief.

But could I do this?

Ironically, I hardly got to say a word to him at dinner. He crammed his food down and went outside to prepare for the square dance. My stomach dropped at the very idea as, once again, childhood memories came flooding back.

But the dancing wasn't so bad. Everyone was messing up, so I wasn't the only one, and soon I was laughing with everyone else. Square dancing was also a lot more work than I thought. Vincent do-si-doed and allemande-righted us into near oblivion. Through it all, Cole began to watch me again. His eyes were alive, inviting, and I tried to accept it as best I could. How did I make my eyes do what his did? Could he tell?

He found a way to swing through and grab my hand as he went on to another partner, and my whole body shivered in delight at the touch.

Vincent and his crew entertained us into the dark, and that was when I really began to look for Cole.

I couldn't find him anywhere. I couldn't figure out where he'd gone. He'd vanished.

On my second trip out of the dining room, I thought I caught a glimpse of him in the parking lot in front of the main building. What was he doing there? Was that him?

I stepped down off the porch and got a little closer.

He was talking to someone. Who?

Maybe I should have left, but I couldn't help myself. I had leapt off a cliff, and I had to take it to its inevitable destination, good or bad.

It was hard to see what was going on because the only light was the one over the porch doors, but as I crept closer, I saw Cole was with a man.

A big one.

And they were holding each other.

I froze. Were they kissing?

No.

I had to be imagining it. Cole said he wasn't seeing anyone.

Then I saw Cole try to pull away, but the bigger man wasn't letting him. *What the fuck?*

I moved ever closer and could hear Cole. "No, Garrett. Let me alone."

"But, dumplin', I *love* you!"

"You don't love anyone except yourself," Cole said, pulling away again. "Now please, leave."

But the big man wasn't leaving. He reached out, grabbed Cole, and yanked him close, crushing his face against my wrangler's. Cole was struggling, but obviously the big man was stronger.

"Argh!" Cole cried. "My God. You *bit* me."

"Want to make us the same."

"Jesus! Get the fuck away from me."

"What's going on?" I shouted, turning my steps into a full run.

The big man spun. I could barely see him in the light from the porch, but the moon was rising over the trees, and I could see he was much older than Cole. Somewhere between forty and fifty, and he had a graying beard.

"What the fuck?" Garrett said.

"Neil, get out of here," Cole called out.

Before I even knew what I was doing, I pushed the man. Hard. He staggered back and nearly went over, but managed to regain his balance.

"Get away from him," I yelled.

I only had time to register that Garrett was swinging at me before the meteor of his fist hit my mouth and sent me flying back against one of the cars. My head struck the car roof, and I saw stars. Then the man grabbed me.

"No" came Cole's scream and he was on Garrett's back. The man shrugged Cole off like a rag doll, sent him tumbling to the ground, and Garrett came back at me.

The rage surged out of me like a force of nature. For years, I'd held back from the world. I'd been afraid, been scared, but not now. Time seemed to slow down again. Just like it had with my mother. The man was moving in slow motion, but the time warp didn't seem to be affecting me.

The second time the fist came toward me, I ducked under it as if it were hardly moving. Then I was up and my fist was flying. I caught him on the jaw, and he staggered back with a cry of surprise. He came back, though it didn't matter. Somehow, I was Spider-Man or something, and I swung with my other fist, catching him again. It ended with my first punch deep into his gut.

With an "*Oooomph!*" Garrett hit the ground.

Cole had managed to get to his feet and was at my side. "Neil! What are you doing? Get away before he hurts you."

Time resumed its normal speed, and it was as if it had turned its favor from me. Garrett was on his feet in an instant and, to my shock, he spit at me. The wetness struck my cheek, and I wiped it away in disgust. The man was clearing his throat again, hocking up more spit.

"Neil, run! He's got AIDS!"

What?

Time froze again. The night went mute; the darkness even darker.

Then I was falling as Cole launched himself against me, sending us both in a tumble to the ground.

Garrett loomed up over us and raised a foot. "Oh, you messin' with the wrong man."

"Stop!" came a shout before the night was split open by a boom.

We all turned to see Vincent Clark on the steps of the porch. He was holding a shotgun.

"You, Mr. Granger, need to get the hell out of here before I blow your head clean off your shoulders!"

The gun was now pointed out and not up. And anyone who knew Vincent knew what kind of shot he was.

Garrett snarled at the man and started in his direction with a shouted "I'll take that away from you, old man," and then froze at the unmistakable sound of the gun being cocked.

"I mean it," Vincent said. "Darla's already calling the police. You better skedaddle before I make that moot."

Garrett wavered, clearly confused by the turn of events. This was obviously not going how he'd expected. "You fucking old man! I'll come back and...."

I stood, pulling Cole with me, and stepped in front of him. "I don't think that would be a good idea," I said, surprised at the rumble in my own voice. "When the police get here, I'm pressing charges."

Garrett spun. "Oww," he said in a wimpy, whiny voice. "Da big man gonna pwess chawges?"

"Or beat the fuck out of you," I said, taking a step toward him.

"No, Mr. Baxter" came Vincent's voice. "I think I'd prefer to blow him the fuck away. Why, to tell you the truth, it would bring me pleasure."

Garrett spun. Something about those words seemed to shock some kind of sense into him. "I... I'll...."

"You'll *leave*, Mr. Granger," said a new voice. It was Darla, and she stood by her man. She had a gun as well.

I smiled.

She was wearing one of her cowgirl outfits. Pink. As usual, she didn't look ridiculous. And right then she didn't look adorable either. She looked dangerous.

"The police are on their way," she said, a rumble in her voice too. "This is done."

"Fuck y'all," Garrett said again and turned toward me. He started to make a hocking sound again, and we heard the second gun cock.

That was all it took.

Garrett turned and ran. He climbed into his truck—of course it was a truck, and it was huge. It roared into life, and he was gone.

WE WERE in the dining hall, surrounded by family and friends. Darla had herded the guests out, and Cole was kneeling in front of me, holding a bag of ice wrapped in a towel against the side of my face.

"Tell me he didn't spit in your mouth," Cole said, but it sounded more like pleading. "Your eyes?"

I shook my head. "No. He didn't."

I looked at my hand and saw a brownish-red smear. *Is it blood?* Was it Garrett's?

"Was he your old boyfriend?" I asked Cole.

His eyes filled with shame, and he looked down, pulling the ice from my face. "Yes," he whispered.

"And he has AIDS?"

"Yes," he said.

I had to strain to hear him.

"Cole?"

He didn't look up until I asked him to, and when he did, his eyes—those beautiful eyes that had first grabbed my attention on a website—were filled with sadness. I noticed his lower lip was swollen. I reached out, touched it, ran my thumb along it, and he winced. "Stick it out," I said, a tremor of fear tickling through me.

"Huh?"

"Your lip. Stick it out."

He shoved his lip out, and I gently pulled it, not wanting to hurt him any more than he already had been. Relief washed over me. "He didn't break the skin."

Cole closed his eyes, and I heard a hitch in his throat.

"That was insane," I said. "What was that about?"

Cole gave a long, shuddering sigh. "You said it. That was my ex. He came here to…. He wanted me back."

I shook my head. "That was the man you were with two years ago?"

"Yes."

"Give me the ice," Amy said. She had crouched down next to Cole, and he handed it to her without contest. "You okay, Cole?"

"Yes. But Neil. Garrett hit him."

"Neil is a hero," said Vincent, now also standing over us. "And he's welcome around here anytime."

Amy placed the ice pack where Garrett's magnificent blow had hit me like a freight train. I flinched, then let the cold settle against me once more.

"I can't believe you did that, Neil," she said. "*You*. You ever been in a fight in your whole damned life?"

"No. But that man was hurting Cole."

A small smile crept across her mouth. "No halfway with you, is there? All or nothing?"

I blushed.

"What's she talking about?" Cole asked.

"Never mind," I replied. "What was Garrett doing to you?"

Cole shuddered again. "He said he wanted me back. Said we'd shared everything there was for two men to share, but he wanted to give me AIDS so we could have that together too."

My mouth fell open. It seemed impossible. How could people be like that?

"Thank God *you're* okay," Cole said. "I don't know what I'd have done if he'd've hurt you."

"What does God have to do with it?" I said, unable to help it. I'd been angry with the Big Man too long. You just can't let go of something like that overnight.

"I think He brought you to me, and then He protected you."

"That's crazy," I said.

"Neil...." Amy sighed.

"Nevertheless, that's what I think," Cole said.

"You really believe in Him, don't you?" I asked.

"I do," he said with utter conviction. I could see it in his eyes.

Oh, those eyes, I thought. I reached out and touched his cheek, felt a quiver, and gooseflesh ran up my arm.

I had never wanted to kiss anyone more in my entire life. My family—Amy, my daughter, my nephew and niece—plus the owners of Black Bear surrounded me, and I didn't care. I wanted to kiss him. Feel those lips against mine.

"That was the police on the phone," Darla said, sticking her head back into the dining room and breaking the moment. "They got the bastard."

Cole began to shake, and before I knew what I was doing, I pulled him into my arms. "You're okay," I whispered into his ear. "You're okay. He can't hurt you now."

"He sure can't," Darla said.

Apparently, she didn't have old-lady ears. Bionic, maybe. "Told them we're pressing charges. Assured them you would too, right, Mr. Baxter?"

I looked up over Cole into her eyes. "Neil," I said. "Please call me Neil."

DARLA AND Vincent took Cole away after that. When they pulled him away, I almost cried out. I didn't want to let him go. I could have held him forever.

Then it was just me and Amy and the kids. Crystal hugged me, and then she looked at me in awe. "Pop, you're the best."

"I am?"

"Yes!"

How long had it been since my teenage daughter had hugged me so tightly? I couldn't remember the last time she did it at all.

"That really was pretty cool, Uncle Neil," Robin said.

I couldn't help but be pleased. With teenagers, someone my age has usually passed out of being "really cool" a long time ago.

Even Todd added his opinion. "Dude, wicked." He nodded. "That was dope."

I hoped that meant something good.

And then Crystal hugged me again.

I held her in my arms. I think Emily would have been pleased.

When Crystal finally relaxed her hold, she still didn't let go. She looked me deep in the eyes. "You like Cole, don't ya, Pop?"

I went stiff for a second, then calmed down. She couldn't mean what it sounded like. "Why, of course I do, dear," I murmured and patted her shoulder. When she pulled back, the joyful look on her face made me wonder what was going on in her head. And then for a moment, I was struck by how much she reminded me of her mother at that age.

It warmed my heart.

Emily lived on in Crystal.

That was life.

"You guys ready to get out of here?" Amy asked us.

"Yeah, I think I am," I replied. "It's been a big night."

"It's been a big *day*," she said.

She took my hand and walked me outside onto the porch. There was a gentle wind stirring the wind chimes. Crystal gave me one more hug, and then she and Robin and Todd ran off into the night.

"Not exactly how I was picturing the evening ending," I said.

"*Ooohh*," Amy said, and, by goodness, she giggled. "What *had* you planned?"

"Oh, relax," I said, my face blazing.

Amy leaned against me, and I was struck again by how small she was next to me. Her head rested right up against my chest. Cole's would come a bit higher. My shoulder, I think.

"Gonna be a full moon," she commented, looking up at the sky. "Tomorrow night, I think. Or the next."

"Yup." I smiled. Put an arm around her shoulders.

"You really okay?" she said.

"Yup," I said again.

"Good," she replied. "Because I'm worn the hell out and I'm hitting the sack."

"Me too." I bent to kiss her forehead.

"Love you," she said.

"Me too," I replied.

WHEN I was lying in bed, the moonlight pouring through the window, I couldn't help but think of Cole. How *had* I thought the evening was going to end? With him here with me? Was I ready for something like that? That big a step? I felt a stirring as my penis began to get hard at only the thought of him in my bed. Obviously my cock thought it was a good idea. It had never filled so fast with thoughts of anyone else.

"My God," I whispered. I was seriously considering the idea of taking someone to bed again.

I was seriously considering taking a man into my bed.

Then I realized with a gasp that I'd let the word "God" pass my lips again.

Maybe you're not done with me, Old-Timer, I thought. And entertaining that idea: *Okay. Let's see what you have in store.*

Then I let thoughts of God pass from my mind.

I thought of Cole.

I thought of him in this bed.

I conjured up our dream kiss.

And I took my now very hard cock in hand.

It didn't take long.

I WAS in the hot tub again. I'd woken up early and known there was no way I was going to be able to get back to sleep. No way at all. It was still a couple of hours before anything was planned. I thought the schedule had said it was a canoe trip ending back at the ranch. So with time to spare, I was back in the hot, bubbling water to which I'd become addicted.

I realized I was going to have to get a hot tub. I'd heard they were a lot of work, but it would be worth it. Not a big one. Just a small one like this. Big enough for one.

Or two?

That made me think of Cole, and I smiled. What had the little son of a gun said? *"You can get nekkid. I could come keep you company."*

I was getting hard once more. I felt like a kid. Was I going to have to jerk off again?

Save it.

For what? I asked myself, and by goodness if I didn't feel my face redden, even though I was alone! I'd embarrassed myself. I laughed, and it felt good to laugh. To really, really laugh. I let it out. I suddenly wanted to jump up and dance.

Then I heard a sound.

It was weird.

Sort of a gurgling. A warble.

What the hell could that be? I wondered.

I will never understand why I did what I did next. My arms were crawling, the hair on the back of my neck sticking up as I got out of the hot tub and looked around.

"Hello?" I called, ignoring what I know now was a premonition. Of self-preservation. If it had been a movie, I would have been screaming at the hero to go in the house. But I wasn't in a movie. This was real life. And I was born and raised a city boy. I guess my sense of preservation wasn't nearly as tuned as it could have been.

There it was again… what? A grunt?

Unlike in the dream, I wrapped myself in a towel. Strange how in just a few days I could be so comfortable with nudity, but what I heard was coming from the other side of the fence. The last thing I wanted to do was walk in naked on a couple making love. And that was a lot what the grunting sounded like. Sex.

There was another strange warbling sound. "Hello?" I called out again, and it was answered by another one of those gurgles.

Just like in my dream, I went to the gate and opened it.

And just like in the dream, there was a bear outside the gate.

It was indeed black, although some part of my brain noticed its snout was brown.

It was indeed big.

Very, *very* big.

Its mouth opened wide, and it looked big enough to swallow me whole. The teeth were huge, and it growled.

"Oh" was all I could say before my throat seized up.

The animal grunted, growled again, and rose up. And up. And up.

It was the second most terrifying moment of my life. I couldn't move. My brain wasn't working. It was trying to. I was trying to make it work, but it refused to cooperate. What was I supposed to do? Hadn't Darla or Vincent or someone said something?

Something about how black bears don't like humans and rarely approach them. Was I supposed to flap my arms? Was I supposed to play dead?

Run, my brain finally screamed as it raised its arm, showing claws just as big and just as sharp as those belonging to the great stuffed bear in the dining hall.

I'm going to die.

Unfair!

Not now.

I thought all of that, as goofy as it seemed later.

And then, just as I was about to slam the gate, I saw Cole there behind the bear. Where had he come from? And he had a rifle at his shoulder!

"Don't move, Big Daddy," he said, and the bear whirled around. There was a boom that tore the day apart, a high-pitched scream—*oh my God, it got Cole! It's killing Cole!*—and then a second boom.

And just that fast it was over.

The bear fell back, crashing into the side of the fence that, for some wild reason, didn't shatter from its weight. A small part of my mind saw that Cole was doing his miraculous rapid emptying and reloading of the rifle even faster than he'd done at the tournament. It was a good thing, too, because then the great animal cried out, a horrible noise—the noise I'd mistaken for Cole's death cries, I realized later—lifted up, and was hit by the third shot.

With one last cry, the bear slumped to the ground and did not move.

I began to shake and watched, as if it were a movie, as Cole ran toward me, literally leapt over the bear, and grabbed me. I threw myself into his arms, shaking so hard I don't know how I didn't break apart.

"I've got you, Neil," he said. "I've got you. It's okay. You're safe now." All this time he was rocking me, murmuring into my ear, stroking my hair. He pulled me tighter, and I molded myself against him, some part of me registering I'd underestimated his height. He was shorter than me, but not by much.

"I—I am?"

"He's dead."

"A-are y-you sure?" I couldn't stop stammering. My teeth were almost chattering.

He pulled back just enough to look at me with his beautiful eyes. "Do you trust me?"

I nodded, and then he pulled me tight again. At first, I thought I might cry, but that urge vanished quickly. I think I must have cried myself out the day before.

I was overcome by a sense of safety like I had never known in my life. Cole had me. He'd protected me, saved me. I wrapped my arms around him tighter, marveling at how hard his body was. It felt nothing like Em's. There was no softness here at all. This was a man. It felt so good. *He* felt so good. So right. Nothing had ever felt so right.

I realized I was getting hard. And there was no way he could miss it.

Cole pulled back slightly and looked deep into my eyes.

Now we're going to kiss, I thought. *At last.* I started to close my eyes and leaned forward.

"Daddy," he whispered, "you better get dressed."

"Dressed."

"Ya dropped your towel."

I stepped back, and sure enough, my towel was on the ground. When had that happened?

I was standing there naked before Cole.

My cock stood half hard before me. Cole was looking. His cheeks reddened.

"God," he said.

I started to cover myself, and then dropped my hands at my side instead. I wanted him to see me. I wanted to see if he wanted me.

"God, you're beautiful," he said.

"You are," I replied, and he looked up at me in surprise, his throat working.

"Neil, as much as I would like to keep staring at you, there are going to be people here any second. And as much as I'd love to take you up on it, I think this better wait."

"People?" I asked.

He nodded. "The rifle. Three shots? They're going to be here any minute."

"God," I said—and there I was using that word again—and I ran inside to get my clothes.

It wasn't a moment too soon.

Vincent and several wranglers were there by the time I made my way back outside.

"Looks like we got us *two* goddamned heroes" was the first thing Vincent said.

CHAPTER 11
Anticipation

THE REST of the morning turned out to be quite the adventure. Everyone wanted to see the bear, hear about the bear, hear about how Cole had *shot* the bear. Even the local news station showed up and interviewed us both. Needless to say, his story was more exciting than mine; he was the hero.

It seems Cole had come to see me and saw the bear first. He ran into the front door of my cabin, got the rifle down from over the fireplace—he had the key—then came back around and shot the thing. Good thing, too, because this same bear had been playing havoc upstream and had nearly injured some people. If Cole hadn't shown up when he did, I very well might have been killed. Cole saved my life.

But why had he come to see me?

Was it just to tell me about how my family wanted to go on another early morning hike or horseback ride?

Or could there have been something else?

"You're the one who saved me," he whispered when he got me aside.

Me?

I didn't know about that. I did know something had irrevocably changed between the two of us, though.

There was no canoe trip that day. Instead, the Black Bear crew decided to move the overnight campout to that night.

It wasn't a big deal since there was only a small group involved in actually spending the night on the trail. I was somehow a part of this group, and I *know* Amy had neglected to tell me about it.

Seems the campout was planned so a few daring souls could get the feel of what it was really like to live in the Old West and be on the trail. We'd all go out on a cattle drive, and then dinner would be cooked over an open fire and a few "lucky" guests would sleep in two-man tents on the ground—like in the Westerns, like in the Old West—while everyone else headed back to the comfort of the cabins. We were going to sleep on the hard ground. Not even an air mattress. The only modern consideration we'd have would be a blue nylon tarp under us. Our bedrolls were pretty authentic, though—a large wool blanket doubled over, rolled into a cylinder, and carried with us on our mounts. That's what we'd have to lie on and keep warm under.

I was glad it was such a warm summery night.

"What the hell is my back going to be like tomorrow?" I asked Amy.

She just laughed. "Oh, please! *You* have a hot tub to climb into as soon as we get back. I have no sympathy. And our spa appointment's tomorrow."

And so we herded cattle. Right out to the very edge of the Black Bear property, where we all had a dinner cooked over the fire.

This was less elaborate than our previous meals, as they were trying to give us a "taste" of what we might have eaten a hundred years ago. It consisted of beans, but also a chunky stew filled with beef, onions, and potatoes, and something called fry bread, which was round pieces of dough the size of tennis balls that were flattened and deep-fried in what was probably terribly unhealthy oil.

But it was all eyeball-rollingly delicious. Especially considering how long this day had been. It seemed a year since I'd opened the gate, naked as the day I was born, and stared into the face of that huge bear.

Cole had stuck with me on the trail all day, keeping Maddy close to Mystic so our legs would occasionally bump. I think I had an erection most of the day. And how amazing was that? Had anticipation for something ever been so strong? I didn't think so.

It wasn't like making love with Em had ever been a chore. I loved her, and I think that was the key. We'd known each other for years, but when I went to her the fateful night I fled from my mother's house, something happened. She'd held me while I cried and was with me when the police showed up. She held my hand through all of it, despite the fact the cops didn't want her there. She held her chin out defiantly and dared them to make her leave.

That's when I thought I fell in love with Em.

I *did* love her. I loved her like I had never loved another human being before. It had swept over me like an avalanche. I'd certainly never felt like that for a girl before.

Maybe it was only natural to think it was something more than it was.

That I had somehow been "saved" from my homosexuality.

What I can't figure out is why I felt I needed to be saved.

I'd already given up on God—even before my mother came at me with a knife.

Why did I care?

But I did.

The very idea of being with a man again.... It scared and thrilled me at the same time.

I would think about Rod...

...and I would think about Mom and her belt and being taken away for a few weeks.

I would think about the exciting night skinny-dipping at church camp with George...

...and I would think about being caught masturbating with him and them sending him away and the terror Mom would find out.

I would think about Jack and how hot it was a "straight" man had sucked me off... how he had come to me and told me that he wanted to continue having sex with me!

And I would think about Mom coming after me with a knife.

But now? Somehow I was finally beyond all of that. Like a historian, I could look on these incidents as stories from a distant past. Finally, they seemed to have lost their hold on me. Was I free at last?

It had all happened so fast!

All day long I had ridden alongside this wonderful man. A man who made no excuses for who he was—a masculine, strong, confident man. He wasn't anything other than who he was. And he was making no excuses for who he wanted.

He wanted me.

And I wanted him. I wanted him so much.

When the time came, would I be able to do it? Would I panic? Would the fear come back?

I realized I'd better tell him at least some of my history.

And so I did. In bits. In snippets. When there was no one around who could hear.

"My God," he said and reached out to me. To my surprise, I reached back, not caring who could see us clasp hands and tangle fingers. "Now I think I understand."

At some point, Crystal and Robin rode up beside me, giggling like girls half their age.

"Cole and Pop (Uncle Neil), sitting in a tree," they sang. "K-I-S-S-I-N-G!"

I know I blushed then ten times more than any other time that week, which was saying a lot.

Cole talked too, telling me about Garrett and how, at first, it was the relationship of his dreams. It had started as something physical. Garrett couldn't have been more his type—over twenty years older, hairy, taller. They'd fallen in love.

Suddenly, any worries I'd had about the difference in our ages were gone. And funny how he preferred body hair, and I had always been attracted to men with smooth chests.

How nice it worked out....

Then Cole told me the bad part. They'd been a couple for over three years when he found out Garrett was cheating on him. "Big-time," Cole said. "He was a favorite in Little Rock, and he traveled a lot. Met men online from all over his territory and fucked them. What's weird was he'd let them fuck him. Never me. I had never minded, though, because I am pretty much a big ol' bottom."

"Big old bottom?" I asked, and when he turned bright red, I figured it out.

I'm sure I turned twice as red as he had.

He cleared his throat and went on. "So Garrett let these guys fuck him. And he wasn't safe."

I looked at him and didn't say a word.

"He didn't make them wear condoms."

"And it's how he got infected," I said. It wasn't a question.

Cole nodded. "HIV. We weren't safe together. I didn't think we needed to be. We were at a gay pride event a couple of years ago and we got tested as usual and...." Cole sighed, looked away, and I reached out and took his hand.

"It's okay," I said. "It's in the past. Let it go." I was already echoing Amy's words. Amy's very, very good words.

"Only that time he tested positive. Turns out he'd been positive for months. We suddenly remembered the week where he'd had night sweats, but I'd had the flu the week before, and we'd never thought anything of it. Neil, I was so fucking scared. They were pretty surprised I tested negative. He'd been fucking me almost every night. He always had.

"Garrett said he was happy for me. Said he was relieved. He'd felt so bad. But there was something in his eyes....

"So they figured, the doctors, they'd better send off my test the second time. The first time we'd taken the one where they can tell in less than a half hour. It's pretty accurate, but not *as* accurate. For the second test, they sent my blood away to a lab, and the next two weeks were a living hell. Thank God Darla snuck me some Valium. I got through the two weeks, and it came back negative. I didn't believe it. I demanded they test me again. They said they didn't need to, that I should wait three months, but fuck that. I wasn't waiting. So they tested me again, and it came back negative again.

"Now get this. That's when I find out Garrett is *still* cheating on me. Without condoms! The fucker is out there, knowingly spreading it around! That was it. I kicked his ass out and moved out of the cabin. The... ah... cabin you're staying in."

"What?"

"I built it. Pretty much on my own, with a little help at the end from Garrett. I'd done most of it before we met. But after we were over, I couldn't stay there any longer. I moved back into the big house—the ranch house, where Darla and Vincent live—and began working on another cabin. I moved into it last fall. Wait until you see it. It's twice as big. Has a real kitchen and everything."

"So you live here year-round?"

Cole nodded. "Of course. Darla and Vincent are my aunt and uncle."

"What?"

I couldn't have been more surprised.

The conversation in Darla's office suddenly made more sense.

Vincent and I love him very much. He's family.

I hadn't realized she'd meant it literally.

"You know, I pretty much stopped believing in God there for a while, Neil."

That caught my attention. I actually jerked in my saddle. Mystic didn't like it and told us both so. "You stopped believing in God?" I asked. *Just like me.*

"Couldn't figure out how He could've let all that happen to me. Give me love, only to have it turn out that the man He gave me was a cheater who, for all intents and purposes, had tried to kill me. I was through with Him."

I nodded. "I understand!"

We urged our horses on before we fell behind.

"And I was through with love too, I'll tell you. For a while. When I finally thought I might try again, I was too scared. I was afraid I still might have HIV, you know? And what if I gave it to someone? I couldn't live with myself if I did that.

"But recently, about four months ago, I had my two-year anniversary of testing negative. The doctor said I couldn't be much more assured I was out of danger."

"Oh, Cole," I said, thrilling at his words.

"I just couldn't believe it," Cole said. "I asked the doctor how it could be, and you know what he told me?"

I shook my head. "No," I whispered.

"He told me it was a miracle."

A miracle, I thought.

"You know what happened then?"

"Tell me!"

"You're going to say I am crazy."

"Tell me," I urged him. Now I had to know.

"I heard a voice." A beatific smile spread over Cole's face. "In my head."

That sent goose bumps up my back and down my arms, making the hair stand up.

If I had ever thought Cole was beautiful before, now he was transformed into something even brighter, lovelier.

"Clear as I am talking to you now," Cole said, "the voice asked me if I could believe again now."

I pulled back on Mystic's reins without even realizing it, and we stopped once again.

"I knew then that God was real," Cole stated.

I stared. What could I say? For a moment I wanted to reject what he was suggesting. That it was "God" who had spoken to him.

"You think I'm crazy, don't you?" Cole said.

But then, to my surprise, I realized I didn't.

For the first time in years, I began to wonder if maybe, just maybe, I could open my heart and believe in "something" once again.

IT WAS during a little break that Cole kissed me the first time.

He led me off into the woods and pressed me against a tree. He looked at me. Just looked at me. I fell into his deep brown eyes.

"I want to kiss you, Neil."

I tried to answer, but my vocal cords just froze up.

"And I think you want me to kiss you."

I still couldn't talk, but I could nod. And I did.

He smiled that beautiful smile. "Do you trust me, Neil? Because I trust you."

I trembled. "Yes," I told him.

And he kissed me.

He finally kissed me.

My head went light, my knees went weak, and I might have fallen if not for the tree. And Cole's hard body pressed against me. His man's body. God.... I was being kissed by a man. At last, at last, at *last*.

I'd met him only a few days before, but it felt like I had waited forever. Maybe I had. It was the most exciting kiss of my life. It left the one with Jack in the dust—and that had been pretty exciting.

And as I melted against Cole, there was no doubt I was kissing a man. Not only was it more demanding, harder, stronger, but there was his closely cut goatee rubbing against my chin and face. So erotic! I was so hard, my cock hurt. He reached down and rubbed me through my jeans, and I moaned. Then he broke away. He'd touched my lips with his tongue, and I'd opened my mouth to take him in, and instead he stopped.

"No," I said with a groan.

"Later, Daddy. Promise."

Later....

It almost made me sad that the kiss was better than any I'd ever shared with Em. But it hit me, the undeniable truth.

"I'm gay," I whispered for the first time out loud.

"What?" Cole said.

I smiled. "I'm gay, Cole."

He smiled back. "Yeah, Big Daddy, I think you are."

I just looked at him. I was choked up. I didn't know whether to laugh or cry.

"Did it feel good to say it?" Cole asked.

I laughed.

"Yes," I said, and I began to tingle all over. "Yes. Yes it did!"

AFTER DINNER, most of the guests left to go back to the cabins. Cole and Cassie and about ten guests remained, including my family. Interestingly enough, there were twelve of us and six tents.

Six two-man tents. Funny how it worked out Cole and I would have to share.

We built up the fire and toasted marshmallows. No conflagration this time, though, and for those who wanted, they could get their treats as perfectly browned as they liked. Amy was in heaven.

It turned out Cole liked his like mine.

He got a little bit in his goatee.

Heart pounding, knowing in our tight little group around the fire I would almost certainly be seen, I wiped the tiny bit of stickiness away with my fingertip. Showed him. Then before I could do anything, he took my hand in his and popped my finger in his mouth. His tongue licked the marshmallow quickly away, and I shivered despite the flames. My cock went as hard as I could ever remember. Our eyes were locked, and I know I had to be blushing. People had to be looking. They had to. My daughter, for goodness sake. And Amy and—*hell!*—Robin and Todd.

But what I saw in Cole's eyes made me not care.

So beautiful....

The moment ended, and I glanced around the fire, but no one seemed to have even noticed—or they were artfully minding their own business.

I took the opportunity to go pee. Cole stuck to the log we were sitting on. Part of me wished he had come with me. Another part remembered that supervisor and knew it wasn't the way I first wanted to see Cole's... to see him naked.

As I was walking back—watching for copperheads!—I heard Todd say, "Hey, Cole! Are we gonna have ghost stories?"

"You bet," he said. He told the classic one about the couple making out in their car and the news report about an escaped murderer called "the Hook" because one of his hands had been replaced with a steel hook. Then them hearing this sound on their roof and being afraid of this hook killer and driving off, engine roaring. And of course the famous ending. The boy getting the girl home and going to let her out of the car and then screaming because, "there, hanging from the car door handle, was a bloody hook!"

"I thought it was the girl who screamed," said Robin.

"Wasn't someone supposed to be hanging from the tree and scratching the roof or something?" asked Crystal.

"I thought the guy got out of the car where they were making out," someone else said. "And then she hears this thump on the roof and it's her boyfriend's head."

"Didn't the killer poke the kid's eyes out?" asked an older lady—Cheryl, I think her name was.

"Oh for goodness sake!" cried Cole. "Who's telling this story?"

So storytelling wasn't exactly Cole's strong point. He would just have to rest on his horseback riding, his shooting, his singing, and... kissing.

With a happy smile, I sat down next to him, very close, so I could nonchalantly put my arm behind him. Not exactly around his shoulders, but he felt it and leaned into it. It made me feel a little possessive.

I liked the feeling.

Cole looked at me and smiled. "What're you thinking about, Big Daddy?" he whispered.

Kissing him. That was what I was thinking about.

And more. A lot more. I was so excited. My cock was hard. And I was terrified.

"You," I managed to whisper back.

"All right, it's my turn," said Cassie, the cute blonde girl I'd met when we first got to camp. She rolled up her sleeves. "Let an expert have a try."

Everyone clapped. I wasn't sure why.

Until she told her story.

"Once, not far from here, in fact," she said, "on a summer night, there was a family, camping... *just* like us." Cassie, her normal smiles gone to be replaced by a very serious expression and wide eyes and raised brows, told a chilling story about campers being abducted by aliens, and when she was done, we all applauded.

"And that's how it's done," she said, winking at Cole.

"Not fair." He turned to me. "Our little Cassie Shell here is an aspiring writer. She sold her first story this year."

"It's a small publisher," she said, and was that a blush I saw? It was hard to tell by the firelight.

"Small or not, it was accepted. And that's a pretty big deal."

Then Cole broke out his guitar, and we sang around the campfire. It might have been corny if it hadn't been so much fun.

Cole was so gorgeous in the firelight. Have I said that before? How he looked in the orange-gold light, his dark eyes all but lost in shadow? Have I said what a good voice Cole has? How strong and clear and kind it is?

Should I mention the laughter when he changed the lyrics of "Home on the Range" to "where the deer and the antelope are *gaaaaaaay*"? I suddenly saw there wasn't a person there who didn't know he was gay and cared one way or another.

Everyone there loved him.

My God! Everyone.

Me.

And then he sang another song by Christine Kane.

"Dream and the way will be clear," he sang. "Pray, and the angels will hear." Turning to me, he sang, "Leap and the net will appear."

Was there anyone there who didn't know what he was telling me?

I scanned the faces around me. All attention was on Cole. No one was even glancing my way.

No, that wasn't true.

Amy was looking. She was smiling. *I love you*, she mouthed silently, and my heart skipped.

I returned her smile and then looked at Cole.

So handsome.

Was I really, possibly, maybe, going to…?

After about an hour, Cole stood up, stretched like the worst actor on the planet, and said with a mighty yawn, "Well! I am durned *tuckered* out." He leaned his guitar against a log. "Been a *loooooong* day! Bear killin' and cattle herdin' takes it out of you, ya know? Anyone wants to play my guitar, they're welcome."

He pushed at his back and, to be fair, we all heard it pop. Several times.

"You go to bed, you," Amy said.

Cole nodded and looked at me so hard it's a wonder I didn't burst into flames. "See you later?" he asked.

I gulped.

Cole walked the short distance to our tent, turned and gave me one more look, nodded, then crawled into our shelter.

The flap closed. I just sat there. I couldn't move.

Finally, Amy leaned over and whispered, "Babe, if that boy wanted me, I wouldn't be sitting here around this fire."

"Amy," I whispered. I shot my eyes back and forth between her and Crystal and the others, all only a few feet away.

Amy shrugged.

"Have you looked at those tents? Everyone will hear us."

Just then there was the sound of Cole's guitar being strummed, and then a woman's voice rang out clear and loud. If Crystal had been paying me any attention at all, it was now totally diverted to the woman's singing.

Amy smirked and gave me a big shrug. "There," she said. "Ask and you will receive. Just don't make *too* much noise."

CHAPTER 12
Making Love

THE WALK to our tent was the longest walk I'd ever taken. My heart was threatening to pound right out of my chest.

Could I do this?

Could I not?

I glanced over my shoulder, but Amy's back was turned. She was singing, and I had no idea what song it was. I glanced around the ring of people. Not one person was looking.

So what was I waiting for?

I went to my knees and pushed the tent flap aside. Would I even be able to see? My first time making love with a man and would I have to play it all by touch? Be totally silent? I mean, Crystal was right outside. I couldn't make too much noise. My heart hitched. I wanted to see Cole's face. The eyes I had fallen for. His chest. I'd been so curious about his chest. And yes, his cock and the ass I'd been staring at encased in his always almost ridiculously tight jeans.

"At last," Cole whispered.

"Cole," I said. "What about the kids?"

"*Shhhh*," he hushed.

I didn't want to be shushed. I wanted to be assured. And I didn't want, when I was finally letting myself free to truly be with another man, for it to all happen in the dark—in the cramped space inside a small pup tent.

But then, even though there was only a small amount of light making its way into the shadows of the tent, it sparked off Cole's eyes, and I knew it would be all right.

I crawled in, letting the flap close behind me, and a second later, Cole's lips were on mine. It lasted all of a few seconds before he broke our kiss, teasing me again with his sweet lips. I nearly cried out in frustration.

"Come on," he whispered and took my hand.

"What?" I said.

"Do you trust me?"

"Yes."

Then we were crawling out the back of the tent. Cole rose, reached out his hand, and helped me to my feet. He pulled me close, and I could see his grin in the outer reaches of the firelight.

"Come on," he said.

"Where?" I responded.

"*Shhhhh!* Trust me," he said, and he turned and pulled me along with him.

We went through a break in the trees and were plunged into darkness.

"There's a slight drop here, so be careful," Cole said and shepherded me into the black. I felt the drop, and it was okay. "Now a root right around…. Here it is." Yes, and I made it over that too. We eased down the slope, Cole's hand never leaving mine.

Then there was light.

We had come into a clearing, and the full moon, the one Amy had speculated on only the night before, was beaming down on us, bathing us in its blue-white light. There was a little pool of water there, catching a reflection of the silvery moon. Cole let go of my hand and backed away. He smiled. I could see his smile.

He kicked off his boots, bent to pull off his socks, and then threw them carelessly aside. He flexed his long toes—I could see even his toes in that silver light—and it was so erotic I could scarcely believe it. Toes?

Then he slowly began to unbutton his shirt.

I couldn't breathe as I watched his chest being revealed to me. The moonlight turned him into a Greek statue—Hermes, Apollo. Funny, wasn't it? That only yesterday I had thought Amy looked like a statue. But she had not been bathed in light that made her skin look like marble.

And this statue was coming to life before my eyes.

Cole pulled his shirt open and, God, it was hairless. I couldn't see a one. Yes, moonlight isn't sunlight, but that night? It was like a beam of light from—should I say it?—heaven.

Then the shirt was falling back off his shoulders, and I gasped.

I couldn't believe how big his chest was. Each pectoral looked to me like it was the size of a dinner plate. His nipples were large, the areolas as big as silver dollars, and I wanted to taste them. His tummy was tight, the ridges of the muscles deep. I longed to touch them. His navel was a dark indent. Cole was so hairless there wasn't even a trail down into his jeans. I felt my cock began to leak in my pants, but just when had I become hard in the first place? Back at the fire?

The day in the dining hall when I first met him?

Surely not just four days....

Cole took a deep breath, and I watched his chest expand.

My heart raced at his beauty.

How had I fooled myself for so many years into not knowing that this was what I wanted?

He smiled.

Then he turned, weaving his body slightly like a young tree in the wind. After a series of popping sounds—the buttons of his jeans opening—the waistband of his jeans began to slip. With each grind of his hips, the denim fell lower. *Oh! There!* I got a peek at the top of the cleft of his ass, and bit by bit more of Cole's perfect high cheeks were revealed to me. Then his jeans dropped, and his thighs and full, round, perfect bottom were there before me.

I gasped.

Was Michelangelo's *David* like Cole? My God! What had the master thought the first time his model had posed for him? Was it something like I was feeling right now?

I wanted to fall to my knees.

Cole stepped out of his pants and stood there totally naked. He looked over his shoulder, and again my breath caught.

He raised his hands to his side and then turned slowly and stood nude before me.

Unlike David, my man was erect, full, hard.

I could barely breathe. His cock rose from a nearly hairless pubic triangle—proud, demanding, beckoning me. Cole didn't look quite human standing there in the moonlight, fireflies beginning to dance around him, shadows behind him, the trickling of the creek filling my ears like music, like the wind chimes back at the ranch house. He looked more like something out of a fairy tale.

Had I stopped believing in God?

Who else could have made such beauty?

Trembling, I went to him, and Cole pulled me into his strong arms. He kissed me in a way that made every kiss before it seem like nothing. Nothing. Even his first kiss.

He opened his mouth to me, and his tongue touched my lips. I opened my mouth to him in turn, and his tongue slipped in, stroking, urging, commanding attention.

I responded in a way I didn't know I could. It was like I was falling into Cole, but he was falling into me as well. Our tongues danced against each other, caressing, making love. Our teeth clashed. Oh, the feel of his goatee against the rough day's growth on my own face!

Then Cole was tearing at my shirt. I was sure he was ripping buttons off, and I didn't care. He cast my shirt aside and pulled my hirsute chest against his smooth one. He was gasping.

"My God," he said with a catch in his voice as he stepped back. His eyes were so dark they seemed primeval.

He pushed me against a tree, the rough bark scratching at my back.

"My God," Cole said again "Your chest!" He ran his hands up my belly and out across my pectorals, his fingers combing through the hair. "Oh, Neil," he murmured. "So beautiful...."

Beautiful? Me?

"So damned sexy!"

Sexy? Me?

He lowered his head and took my right nipple into his mouth, and I felt his tongue running around and around its circumference. I bit down to keep from yelling. That woman might still have been singing, the camp well away from us, but they would have heard the shout my soul wanted to cry out.

This was our time.

My time.

I pushed him back. I had to taste too. I had to. I spun him around, shoved him against my tree, and dropped my lips to his chest, kissing, licking it, finding a nipple, sucking it into my mouth. *So* different from Em's. Powerful. Masculine. Waves of energy seemed to be flowing from him into me. Yes, this was how it was supposed to be! I nearly cried in joy.

I let go of his nipple, ran kisses over to the other one, took it into my mouth and sucked. His chest was so muscular, so hard, but his skin was soft as suede.

Cole shouted, and I didn't care. Let them know. I didn't care.

Suddenly, he heaved me back. "Wait! You're gonna make me cum if you don't stop."

I grinned at his words. Had I ever brought out such excitement in another person? All I had done was suck his nipples.

He pulled me against him, and we rubbed against each other, one smooth torso, one hairy.

"The hair on your chest feels so good!"

"Your chest feels so good against mine," I told him. He was feeling this as much as I was, wanting the same thing. He wanted—*he needed*—a man.

He grasped the front of my jeans, pulled at the snap, yanked the zipper open. He dropped to his knees and wrenched them down from my waist. "No," he complained when confronted by my underwear, and then he was jerking them down too. He moaned when my erection sprang out to greet him. I was so hard!

"Oh, Neil," he said, "you're huge."

"I am?" I asked and remembered Jack's words. *"This thing is huge!"*

Was I?

Was I any bigger than Cole? *He* looked huge!

Before I knew it, my cock was in Cole's mouth. The shock was so great I don't know how I didn't pass out. So hot. So wet. So sweet.

Cole's head bobbed up and down along my length, and I marveled at how deep he could take me. I watched and was struck by how real my dream of this had been.

In seconds, I knew I might reach my orgasm—too soon!—and pushed him away. "No, not yet. You!"

I reached down and shoved my hands into his armpits, then dragged him to his feet. I grabbed his hands and pulled them over his head against the tree. Even in his armpits, there was hardly any hair and, as if being directed by someone else, I lowered my face into them. I pushed my mouth into one of his pits, filling my nostrils with the scent of him.

I sucked him deep into my lungs. The perfume of man. I sucked his flesh, tasted him, his sweat. It was tangy on my taste buds, and I sucked until there was nothing left to taste before I switched to the other side.

Cole was sobbing, and the sound was music. When I finished, I looked down between his legs to the monolith rising up to greet me. It stretched, jumped, and then I took it in my hand. God, it was so hot. Like a furnace. And so hard. But soft. Like velvet over steel. And if I had liked the smell of him above, the scent rising from his groin was exquisite. His cock throbbed, and my heart slammed against my rib cage.

Do it!

And so I went to my knees and, *finally*, I took a cock into my mouth.

Nothing had prepared me for such an experience.

Cole's cock was so hot, real, and alive.

I shoved myself down onto him, choking on his length.

"Easy, Daddy," he gasped.

I backed off, went slower this time.

So big, so long.

The taste of him was like sugar and salt, skin and summer.

I sucked. Threw away his caution and thrust my mouth down on him, impaling myself onto him.

He was wet with precum dripping from his slit.

"Stop," Cole begged and shoved me back.

"No!" I wanted his cock. How could he deny me what I'd waited a lifetime for?

He kissed me and then pushed me down on the ground that was warm and soft under my back. The rocks were covered in a bed of soft moss. I wanted to laugh as I realized Cole must have orchestrated this whole scene. Picked the exact site for our camp.

Cole pulled at my jeans, fought with my boots, threw them away to wherever he had thrown his own, tore off my socks, and then, God, he was sucking my toes! No one had ever sucked my toes, and the shocks slamming through me were near orgasmic.

He sucked each one. He licked them, ran his tongue between them, crammed them all into his mouth. He was moaning louder than I was, and I wanted to see what it was like. I wanted to taste his toes too. I started to rise, and he forced me back again, lifted my legs, and then.... *Oh!*

He was kissing me, licking me, in a place where no one had been before. Had I thought the jets of the hot tub felt good against that tight secret spot? His tongue was a hundred times better. Those jets had not prepared me for such wonder. I thought I might die from it. He lifted my legs higher, so high my own erection greeted my lips and I realized I was close to being able to take myself into my mouth.

Pleasure slammed through me again as his mouth attacked my hole. Cole kissed me there, licked, dug in with his tongue, sucked.

This is it, I thought. *This is what it's supposed to feel like. Sex is good!*

I had just been with the wrong sex.

After forever, Cole lowered my legs. I was in a daze as he kissed his way up my torso, my chest, sucked at my neck, and reached my mouth. He hesitated, and I took the choice from him. I kissed him hard. Plunged my tongue into his mouth and tasted myself.

His cock throbbed against me, and I knew I had to have it again.

And could I be brave enough to do what Jack had done for me? Could I let him finish in my mouth? I was scared, but I wanted it too. I kissed down this chest, his marble chest, kissed downward into the valleys of his abdomen. And then I took that hard cock back into my mouth. Somehow I went slower this time, marveling at how wonderful it was to have him, wanting it to last forever. Now and again his cock would give a small pulse, and I could taste the leakings from his erection. I was holding his smooth balls, the scrotum like velvet, and then I wanted to taste him there as well. I let go of his cock and went to his balls, and they were so big. I could only get one in my mouth at a time, and he thrashed as I carefully suckled on them. They were so alive!

"Neil! If you don't stop, I'm going to cum."

Right then I knew I could be as brave as Jack, knew I wanted to give *this* man that same pleasure, and I released the testicle I had been nursing and took his hardness back into my mouth.

"No!" he cried. It was only Cole clawing at my back, then pulling me up into his arms, kissing me, that kept me from finishing him.

Our eyes met. He reached down. Took my cock in hand, and I nearly came.

Then: "Fuck me, Daddy," he begged. "Please, please fuck me."

His eyes were wild and crazy sexy.

"Do… do you have a condom?" I asked. Because wasn't that what I was supposed to ask?

"Do you trust me?"

God, yes, I did. I really did.

I nodded.

"I trust you. Take me. I want you inside me. I want your cum inside me. I need it. So long. Been so long!"

"But don't I need something wet? I don't want to hurt you."

"Daddy, you're so wet, I don't need it," he said, stroking me. "And I want it to hurt."

"No," I said. "I don't want to hurt you!"

Cole was doing *something*—shifting, moving—and then he was pushing me onto my back and then scrambling on top of me. Before I even knew it, he'd plunged himself down onto me. One moment I was in that warm July night air, and the next, deep inside my love.

He was like a wet velvet furnace.

After that, a primal nature as old as mankind took over and, like a man possessed, I began to fuck him. Thrust up into him.

There was no finesse to our first time.

I was an animal. I had no control. I rolled him over and *fucked* him. Pounded into him. Took him.

Made him *mine*.

My orgasm ripped through me like an earthquake. It felt like I was pouring the marrow of my bones into him. Cole was writhing under me, shouting out, and I saw he was cumming too. His seed arced out of him, brilliant white in the moonlight, and splashed down on his face, his smooth marble chest, his tight belly.

And then?

I don't know what.

I think I passed out.

Later, we bathed in the pool of water, its temperature just right. We were kissing, and I didn't ever want to stop kissing him. I was hard once more, and I wanted to hold his cock again, and when I reached down, I saw that he was hard too.

Cole grabbed my length, pulled, and then he had his big hand around both of us. "Look," he said.

I did, and there we were, our cocks alongside each other, and it was one the sexiest things I had ever seen. I gasped at the sight.

Cole started kissing my neck as he jacked us. "I've wanted you so much," he whispered in my ear. "So much. I wanted you from the moment I saw you in the dining hall."

"You did?" I tried to ask through the pleasure rushing through me.

"I saw you from across the room, and I was afraid to come to the table."

I laughed. I couldn't believe it. He was afraid of me? I leaned back and looked into his eyes. "You had me with your picture."

"My picture?"

"On the website for the ranch. I found your picture, and that was it. I didn't know it then… didn't allow myself to know it. But now?" I nodded. "Your eyes and your smile…. You had me then."

We kissed some more before we returned to the mossy bank and lay down so we could suck each other at the same time. It didn't take long. He tried to pull away, but I wouldn't let him. Then he was gushing into my mouth in long, hard jets, and I thrilled at the taste of him. This is what I'd heard the women in the offices I'd worked at complain about so bitterly? How crazy! This was bliss, taking all that he was into me, the blueprint that was Cole, swallowing hungrily. My heart raced that I had been brave enough to do it, to give him that ultimate pleasure, and it soared as well that I had loved it. The taste was so exciting my own orgasm suddenly slammed through me, and I unloaded into Cole's mouth. He swallowed me as eagerly as I had him.

When we could talk, he shifted around, held me close, and said, "I wasn't expecting you to do that."

I smiled. "I had to have you."

Sometime later, he led me back to the tent.

Then I was asleep, spooned up against him. Him. Cole. A man. There was nothing else that body I clutched against me could be.

A man.

Home.

I was home.

CHAPTER 13
Making Good

THE REST of the week was a blur. I know a lot happened, and it was fun.

But what I remember is the nights. And the times Cole found us someplace to make love.

I never slept in my cabin again the rest of my vacation. We didn't want to make love in the bed that had once been his and Garrett's. We moved into Cole's, and he was right. It was at least twice the size of his old one and a showplace, like something that should've been featured in a magazine. This one had a beautiful kitchen with one wall made of stone.

The bedroom had a large brass bed.

THE CANOE trip turned out to be one of my favorite memories. Which was something I hadn't expected. Canoe trips in those far-off church-camp days had been all right, but I hadn't been crushed the year I'd gotten sick and had to stay in my cabin for the day.

Tipping over had been a big part of that. To suddenly find myself, my belongings, the book I'd brought to read that day, all in the water had not been fun. Even putting a book in a ziplock bag didn't mean it was safe. Why, once one had gone rushing off, floating down the river, and I never retrieved it. I can't remember what that book was anymore. I'd found it at the used book store in town and made sure the counselors didn't see it. Something about a yellow fog that had crept out over an English countryside and driven people crazy, making them do all kinds of things. It had made a high school shower room full of boys break into an orgy. I'd used that chapter in a stall in the bathroom to great pleasure. It had even been the inspiration for a game with George....

I wasn't happy to lose that book.

I wasn't happy to get soaked either.

But you came to expect it.

The smart kids wore their swimsuits that day. Of course, that didn't stop you from getting sunburned, but even in those days I tanned quickly.

But the canoe trip at Black Bear Guest Ranch was different.

Of course, the company had something to do with that.

The trip started away from the ranch. We were driven some eight miles along the river to put our canoes in and wound up at Black Bear by dinner. The scenery was stunning. It was like going back in time. We rarely saw anyone else as we traveled lazily down the river. The watery highway cut through forest and great rocky formations, the striations stacked like seemingly infinite layers of cake. The colors ranged from gray rock to massive bluffs of sandstone in reds and pinks and browns, and in some areas they towered high above us. The water was so clear we could see the fish and turtles as we drifted by.

There was such beauty along the riverbanks, but it was Cole in my canoe that made it so wonderful. The shy looks, the smiles exchanged, the pleasure of him showing me his favorite sights along the way.

Sack lunches went with us and provided a long enjoyable break at a great widening of the river around noon. Wide enough that we could swim and cool ourselves from the sun.

But Cole had different plans.

As the others banked their canoes on the shore, Cole held us back. We went to land at what looked at first to be a very rocky area, but that was a trick of the eye. Within twenty feet of shore, helping each other as we went, Cole took me to one of his secret places.

A thousand years ago the river had carved a break in the rock, and I found he'd brought me to a deep, cool watering hole kept clear by the flow of river water.

We sat on a big flat stone and had our sandwiches, apples, and bottled water, and then Cole stood up and stripped and bid me to join him in the natural pool. It was the first time I saw him naked in the bright sunlight. The first time I could truly see him in all his glory.

I had never seen anything more beautiful in my entire life.

How had I not known I was gay?

Then, of course, I knew. I knew how I had kept myself from acknowledging who and what I was. For a while I thought it was a demon. For a while a perversion.

But as I looked at Cole, I knew what I felt for him was no sickness. No aberration. No deviance. What I was feeling was natural. Right.

Beautiful.

And once Cole assured me we had time, I shyly stripped off my clothes—was I the same man who had been uncomfortable about getting naked alone in my hot tub?—and joined him in the water.

It had felt wonderful to be naked in the hot tub.

It was paradise being naked in the cool water.

I never worried once about biting fish or snapping turtles.

We swam together, around each other, like mermen.

And then we made hurried love on that flat rock.

But not too hurried.

Because there was something I wanted to do. Something I hadn't been brave enough to do yet.

It hit me when he climbed out of the water before me, hiking a leg up, showing me a sight that made me almost instantly hard. His balls first, hanging down even though the water had been cool. But more. His stunning, muscular ass split wide, and there was his most secret place. To my surprise, it took my breath away.

As a man, you saw other naked men sometimes. In high school in the shower. At the gym in the locker room. But their assholes? That was something you just didn't see.

I knew I wanted to see it closer.

We were sucking each other when I knew I couldn't wait.

I stopped sucking him and moved so that I could get closer. So I could *see* that tight little puckered ring.

It was lovely.

And right then I knew I wanted to do something that I never thought I would want to do. Before I could begin to think about what I was doing, I pulled his legs wide and pushed them back. Even there he had only the smallest amount of hair, as if to remind me this was a man.

I kissed it.

More.

Tasted it… him. Tangy. Sharp. Sexy. Real.

"Oh my God!" Cole cried.

I don't know how long I kissed and licked and sucked him there. I couldn't stop.

"Neil. Please. Fuck me. Please."

I did.

I didn't last long. Neither did Cole.

I had him on his back by then and looked into his beautiful eyes as I fucked him, and when I came, he shot as well, in great jets between us, covering us both. I collapsed upon him, and his powerful legs wrapped around me.

Paradise.

We were cleaning off when we heard Leo calling to us.

We looked up to see him standing on our rock. I saw the hurt in his eyes, but it couldn't be helped.

"We're getting ready to leave soon. Vincent had me come look for you."

"We'll be there in a few minutes," Cole assured him.

He nodded and left.

"Do you think he saw—"

Cole shook his head. "No."

"He looked so hurt," I said. "I feel terrible."

"No!" Cole put his hands on my shoulders and looked me deep in my eyes. "I don't ever want you to feel terrible about anything we do. Especially what we *just* did. I wasn't expecting that. I love it."

My smile came back. "I loved it too."

"You did?" Cole asked, and I saw the hope and longing in his eyes.

"Yes." And then I kissed him, and we started to get hard, damned our circumstances, and got dressed and joined the others.

We fished, and I even managed to catch a lovely trout. Along with the other fish we all caught, we had a fine dinner.

My spa treatment was something I'll never forget. Imagine my surprise when it was a naked Cole who entered the room and not the masseuse I'd been expecting. He rubbed me in all kinds of places I'm sure would not have been on the agenda otherwise. Used things besides hands and fingers and elbows. When he crawled up onto the table and took me deep into himself, it was all I could do not to scream.

Amy teased me later. She'd been in the next room, and Cole and I had not been as quiet as we thought.

THERE WAS great hilarity when Cole tried to teach me to use a lasso. I was terrible, and, of course, he was an expert. I won't talk about how he talked me into trying on some chaps, how they turned him on, and how I surprised him later that night by presenting myself to him in those same chaps. And nothing else *but* those chaps. *And* what we did with that rope.

I was a little scared at a game Cole wanted to play—being tied down brought back some memories. By the time the night was over, however, they'd been replaced by far better ones.

When the kids had a rodeo, it was only Todd who kept Cole and me there to watch. Nothing too dangerous for the youngsters. No bronco riding or anything like that. But they rode horses between barrels and lassoed calves.

The minute my nephew finished, Cole and I left.

We had to find every opportunity there was to make love.

Because there wasn't much time.

The end of the week was approaching rapidly, and it was something I dared not think of.

I had no idea how I was going to return home alone.

SOME SURPRISING conversations took place as well.

Like the one I had with Crystal.

Hiding what had happened between Cole and me was impossible. We couldn't have hidden it if we'd wanted to, and I didn't want to. I wanted to shout it to the world. Crystal was the only reason I'd held back.

She was the one who came to me over breakfast one morning.

She elbowed me and giggled. "Poppa, Poppa, Poppa!"

"What?" I asked.

She rolled her eyes. "You sure have a funny way of showing you don't like gays."

"Crystal!"

She shook her head.

"Guess you changed your mind about Cole?"

I nodded. "I guess."

"Good," she said. "I don't like the idea of you being alone when I go off to college."

"You don't mind?" I asked, surprised.

"Heck no!"

"But... but... back when that woman from work asked me to dinner, you made me promise to never be with anyone again."

Crystal shook her head. "No, Dad. I made you promise never to be with a *woman* again. I said I didn't want a stepmom. Cole can hardly be my step*mom*, can he?"

I shook my head and tried to figure the logic in that. Maybe it was something only a girl could understand? Maybe I would with time?

But something in what she said struck me.

She didn't want me to be alone when she went to college?

Well, wouldn't I be?

Because I lived in Terra's Gate. And Cole lived on Black Bear Guest Ranch.

Six hours away.

It was one more time that I had to block the thoughts of the rapidly approaching end of my week out of my mind.

Alone.

Soon I was going to be alone again.

And I didn't know how I would stand it.

I WAS pretty surprised when Darla took me aside Saturday morning and asked me what my intentions were with her nephew.

"You have to admit," she said, "I have a reason to be surprised and concerned. Wasn't it just days ago a certain guest came to me saying how uncomfortable he was because Cole was gay?"

I couldn't help but be embarrassed.

"You still the same man?" she asked.

I shook my head. "I don't think so."

We were walking through a big garden, filled to overflowing with flowers and shrubs. Not far away was the big house, and it *was* big.

"Our Cole has been hurt enough, you know? By that son-of-a-bitch Garrett, by his parents—"

"His parents?"

"Didn't he tell you?" she asked.

I shook my head.

"*Hmph*," she muttered, then stopped and looked at me. "Maybe I shouldn't say, but I'm goin' to. They threw him out when he told them he was gay. Threw him right out of the house."

I gasped. Sad. Like me. So much like me.

Darla started walking again. "They didn't even let him pack a bag. He hitchhiked here all the way from Chicago. He'd been comin' to stay for the summer for years, and we loved him, so when he showed up, we gave him a place to stay. Norma, Vincent's sister and Cole's mom, had called and told us he might show up and why. She wanted to warn us, she said. God, I hate that bitch." To my surprise, Darla actually spat.

"So you see, we don't want to see him hurt again. It's why I'm asking your intent."

"I'll be honest with you," I said. "I don't know. It's pretty new, you know? I never expected something like this to happen. And I live six hours away."

"Do you love him?" she asked.

"Darla, I've known him less than a week! I don't know. It's wonderful. But are we in love?" My suddenly pounding heart had an opinion. "Or is this just the newness?" And the second suggestion wasn't one my heart agreed with.

She smirked. "Looks like love ta me. At least on Cole's part. I haven't ever seen him like this."

"Really?" I said, heart soaring.

"*Really*," she said.

"He's so young. I'm so much older than Cole."

"Don't know if you've noticed, but he ain't complaining," Darla informed me. "Neil, do I have to tell you this—Cole *likes* 'em older."

Wow was all I could think.

"Do me this favor?" she asked.

"What?"

"Cole is an adult. He's no kid. He knows—at least on some level—that this might be no more than a summer affair. That you live a long ways away."

Suddenly my heart wasn't soaring. It was aching. It felt like cold stone.

"Be kind? Don't just forget about him? Call him once or twice?"

I looked at her and my eyes welled with tears. "Of course."

She gazed up into the blue sky and said, "You'll be back home in your big city."

I didn't tell her that Terra's Gate was hardly a big city.

"And a whole new world has opened for you. I'm not stupid enough to think you won't be... exploring it." She turned back to me. "But a call or two might be nice."

I nodded.

"I'll call," I promised.

It was hard to put on a happy face when I rejoined my Cole.

My Cole.

At least it felt that way.

We had one more day.

God!

What was I going to do?

I did one thing.

We made love that night in an entirely different way.

"ARE YOU sure?" Cole asked.

"I've never been more sure of anything in my life," I told him.

"It's a big thing," he said. "Are you sure you want to give that to me?"

"Yes," I said. "I told you. I've never been more sure of anything."

It was our last night, and I could hardly bear it. How was I going to go home to... not being with Cole? Since that night we'd made love for the first time, we had spent nearly every moment together. How was I going to be without him?

I tried to remind myself that I hardly knew this young man... and yet I felt I knew him better than anyone I had ever met in my life—I had never felt so close to another human being.

It was why I wanted to give him something so I would never forget him. Like that could happen!

The evening had started with a hayride, and without being blatant, we were able to get quite close sitting back in those hay bales, Cole with his arm behind me, fingers just touching my right shoulder. I so wanted to kiss him, but for goodness sake, my family was sitting right there around us!

The ride ended at the main house, and we had steaks grilled on the fire again, but these were thick and made in heaven. There were baked potatoes to go with it and heaping helpings of real macaroni and cheese. Also baked beans, with big pieces of pork, but I only tasted those. I had plans. And corn! Again with the corn, dripping with butter. Corn bread too, and I was most happy to see I was going to get one last taste of that incredible fry bread.

Then came the bonfire.

Cole and I stayed barely a few moments, and then we snuck off.

"Really?" Cole asked.

"Yes," I whispered.

"I—I'm not small," Cole said, stating the obvious.

I laughed nervously. "I know."

We were lying naked in his big brass bed. We had already fucked. He wanted me the moment we got in the cabin and had me take him bent over the bed, jeans at his knees and boots still on. He couldn't even wait for me to get undressed. So I did it that way, my own jeans open only enough to free my cock. Neither of us lasted for long.

"It can hurt at first...." Those eyes of his were filled with concern and—dare I hope it?—something else.

"You said you wanted me to hurt you," I replied.

"What?"

"The first time I... was in you. You said you wanted it to hurt." I hadn't understood, but if hurting was part of it, then okay. But for something that sounded painful, he sure seemed to love it. I wanted to understand that too. Would I love it? I wanted to. Could you like something that hurt?

Cole nodded. "Yes. I wanted to *know* you were in me. And it had been so long. And the hurting can be part of it. But if it's done right—and you did it right, baby—then it turns into something else."

I nodded. "Yes," I said with a gasp. "I want that. I want to *know* that."

And then he began to kiss me.

Things were different this time. I noticed that immediately. We always somehow needed each other so badly that our sex could be fast and rampant, the desire so deep that we practically consumed each other.

But tonight?

Tonight Cole was showing me a different side of himself. We started slow. He wasn't rushing. He laid me back and leaned over me and then kissed me gently, sweetly, unhurriedly. He made me wait before he opened his mouth to me, wait for his tongue. And when it did come, that tongue was so soft and gentle and light. He cupped my face with his big hand, and soon I was high at his touch.

Finally, the kisses got more urgent, and our tongues dueled and danced together. I could hardly believe the level of need he brought up in me. Then he released my mouth and let his kisses travel down my jaw, my neck, my Adam's apple, my collarbone—sometimes giving little nips, never hard, but not gentle either. He was waking every cell in my body.

I wanted to return the favor, but he was having none of it.

"Not this time, my love," he said and my heart surged.

My love? Had he just said "my love"?

Down, down the kisses went, and watching him, seeing Cole's mouth and lips and face travel over my body, made me want to cum without scarcely being touched! Was this what I had denied myself for so long?

How foolish I had been.

Then he was sucking my nipples, sucking and then taking them between lip-covered teeth, and finally nipping fully, those sharp teeth bringing out a pleasure-pain I had never experienced.

All the while, Cole ran his hands everywhere, causing wave after wave of delightful shivers to run all over my body—ripples of gooseflesh, tingling pleasure without end.

My cock throbbed with need, was so hard it hurt, and ran freely with precum. I would have had no problem taking him, and it always delighted Cole that my leakings were so plentiful and viscous that we never needed some manufactured lubrication.

But me taking Cole was not what this was about.

He reached my cock and then breathed on it, the heat from his breath thrilling and tantalizing, and then… then the bastard passed it by, sparing it not even one kiss, one lick, one touch.

I cried out in frustration, and he chuckled and traveled on.

Now it was my legs and then my knees and calves and ankles(!), and the tops of my "hobbit feet," and finally my toes. Cole sucked each one lovingly and slowly, like ten tiny cocks, and I writhed in pleasure, smacking at the bed now with my open palms.

Then Cole kissed and bit at the bottoms of my feet, and it tickled and felt so damned good. He kissed and nibbled even at my heels and then lifted my legs so he could make love to the *backs* of my knees!

And next he lifted my legs higher, spreading them wide and letting them fall to either side of him, so high that they didn't fall back to the bed but stayed spread out in the air. He gave my tightly drawn balls one long lick… and then bent me back farther… and made love to my ass.

First Cole kissed me *there*, just beneath my balls, spreading outward, then drawing back in… closer… closer. Then he ran his hot, wet tongue fully up and down the cleft of my cheeks, and with each pass, that tongue ran hot and heavy over my asshole. Each time, I jumped. Each time, I cried out.

Finally, he bent me near in half, worked himself up so that his knees and thighs were beneath me. My legs went crazy wide, and he focused on my hole—licking, sucking, probing. Slowly but surely a finger joined his tongue, worked itself into me… gently… gently, at first, and then more demandingly. It buried itself to the first knuckle, then deeper, to the second, wiggling, searching, and….

"*Aaaaaahhhh!*" I shouted. He had found something within me, and as he touched it, massaged it, I thought I would go out of my mind!

Cole stopped, and I cried out in frustration, and then a second finger joined the first. Through it all, he never stopped kissing, licking me there, getting even his tongue deep inside me. The pleasure was almost overwhelming, and each time I thought I would cum, he would back off. A third finger joined the other two, and he squirmed them, jiggled them, waggled them, and—Jesus Christ—I thought I was dying and being reborn….

Then….

He stopped.

I was near sobbing as he let my legs fall down around him. He leaned forward and took me in his arms, and I could feel his cock at my door. He looked at me. Kissed my mouth. I could taste the tang of my body, and it only spurred me on.

"I'm going to fuck you now," he whispered.

"Yes, please," I gasped. "Make me yours."

His eyes widened.

I nodded.

Cole reached down between us and adjusted himself, and then ever so gently… pushed. Pushed again. Again.

"Push out," he said, so quietly I almost didn't hear him. "Like you were going to…."

I understood and tried and—*Oh!*—he was inside me.

For one second there was only surprise, nothing else, and then the pain came.

God!

But not as bad as I'd expected. It dropped to a burn and slowly, slowly, slowly he edged himself deeper inside me: in... backing out... in... backing out.

I could not get over the feeling.

Like nothing else in the world.

So strange and yet—

God.

—things were happening.

Unknown happenings.

And....

Ah!

I opened my mouth to say, "Easy!" He was so fucking *big* and...

...and he *was* easy.

Gentler.

Slower.

It *burned.*

And then... then something clicked. We were looking into each other's eyes, and I suddenly understood that this *was* a part of it, and then I just... *opened* to him.

He slid the rest of the way in and seemed almost as surprised as I was and... I... was... his.

Cole waited a long moment until I nodded and told him, "Now."

He fucked me.

Cole started slow, but I knew I could have none of that and urged him on.

"Fuck me, fuck me. *Fuck* me, Cole!"

And he did. Bit by bit he got faster and faster and finally believed me and *pounded* into me.

I had never known such joy.

We lasted longer than I would have imagined, but soon, all too soon, he shouted and his cock began to jerk, and I could feel him cumming into me. Feel the jets pass through his flesh and into mine. Feel the heat of his semen in me. Filling me.

He grabbed my cock, stroked it once, twice, and then I was shooting—joining him in mutual orgasms—pumping my cum out between us, drenching us….

Never.

Never had I known anything like it.

And then Cole fell down on me, and I wrapped my arms around him, and I was crying and he was crying and then we were laughing and then we were silent and simply held each other and I knew I would never be the same.

But I didn't know how my soul would bear leaving him in the morning.

Because I was his.

CHAPTER 14
Bereft

"WELCOME BACK," Gary, my manager, said. "We missed you."

"Thanks, Gary," I said.

He eyed my black cowboy hat. If he thought it was stupid, he didn't say and I didn't care. Not one bit. Now I understood why Owen had always worn his for the first few weeks after he got back from Black Bear Guest Ranch.

And he hadn't had Cole.

Cole picked out that hat. I reached up and touched it.

Cole said I looked great in it. Like a real cowboy. He said that he meant it. He said, "*Grrrrrrrr!*" What did I care what anyone else thought?

"Place almost fell apart while you were gone. We—I—really am glad to have you back." He looked at the hat again, shook his head (at least he was smiling), and walked off down the hallway toward his office.

I went to the break room to put lunch in the refrigerator. Sliced steak on fry bread. The last of it. And a half ear of corn.

"Hey, Neil!" I turned to a nice-looking young man with bright new-penny-copper hair. Sloan. Fairly new guy. Good customer service rep. He could go places at Horrell & Howes.

"Morning, Sloan."

"The hat looks good."

I smiled. Or tried to. "You think so?" I asked. *You're not laughing at me?*

He leaned in. "You look *really* good in it," he said conspiratorially, and then I realized something else. He meant it. He wasn't talking to me dude to dude. I saw it in his twinkling eyes.

God. Sloan was gay.

How the hell had I not known it?

Because you blinded yourself to knowing.

"You look like a real cowboy."

The words jolted me. Cole's words.

"Thanks, Sloan."

He nodded. "I think that dude ranch did you good."

"It did," I said quietly.

"I got to get to my station," he said and gave me a wave and went down an aisle of the phone-rep cubicles.

"Have a good day, Sloan," I called after him.

Gay.

And I didn't think he'd been coming on to me either. It wasn't like that supervisor at the urinals looking at my dick—showing me his. This was more like… camaraderie.

He smiled and reached for a hat that wasn't on his head, tipped it like a gentleman.

I found myself smiling. A tiny ray of sunshine in an extremely gloomy day.

I went to my office and hung my hat and then opened my backpack. It made me more comfortable than using a briefcase. I think it made me less "removed" from those I supervised. I didn't want to be the kind of leader Shelia would have been, treating my employees like I owned them. I'd hated it when I was treated that way through the years, and I thought, *I'm not going to do it to anyone else.* I knew they'd appreciate it.

From the backpack, I withdrew an envelope, took out several pictures from my trip, and pinned them to the corkboard on the wall to the right of my desk. Me and Amy and the kids, my cabin, me and Crystal on our horses, and finally, one of me and Cole. He had an arm around my shoulder, and we were both wearing cowboy hats and cowboy shirts. It wasn't an obvious picture—we could have been friends—but what made me smile was the knowledge that it was a "selfie," and what couldn't be seen was that neither of us had been wearing pants. My special secret.

Someone knocked at the door, and I turned to see Shelia standing in my threshold. I took a deep, quiet breath.

"Good morning, Shelia."

She eyed my hat, and I couldn't help but notice the flash of distaste that crossed her face. She buried it fast. It might have been my imagination, but I didn't think so. And dressed the way she was—and it was extremely professional; she always looked good—I wasn't surprised. That and the fact that she hated me.

A week in a place that loved me—really loved me—and that wasn't just counting Cole. And now, five minutes back and I was already getting some toxicity.

I fought the urge to sigh.

"How can I help you?"

She squared her shoulders.

"Well, as you know, while you were gone, Gary put me in charge…."

Yes, I knew. And why a man as smart as he was did such a stupid thing, I didn't know.

I nodded.

She stepped forward and placed a folder on my desk. I looked down at it. She didn't even hand it *to* me.

"It came to my attention that a number of your employees are breaking company rules. I think it is important that they know that can't be tolerated. Rules exist for a reason. Without them there would be chaos."

I was fighting the sigh, fighting the sigh, fighting the sigh.

"Oh?" I asked. This couldn't have waited? No "Good morning, Neil"? No "Did you have a nice trip, Neil"? No "I like the hat, Neil. It makes you look like a real cowboy"? No "*Grrrrrrrr!*"?

I didn't pick up the folder, and she lifted an eyebrow.

"Don't you agree?"

"I think it depends on the situation, but yes," I said. "Rules exist for a reason." They were, as far as I was concerned, probably different reasons than hers. "Can you give me an idea, though? I have a few things I have to deal with first. Payroll for one."

"Well…," she said, nodding, setting her faux-pearl earrings swaying, "that is important." She straightened her jacket. "Well, Sloan, for instance."

Sloan?

She nodded again, vigorously, the earrings dancing now. "He used the company fax machine. And Charleen. She made some photocopies. And Thomas." She stepped closer to my desk and lowered her voice. "He printed some—" She cleared her throat and that distasteful look flashed across her face again. "—pornography from the Internet."

I am sad to say my eyebrows shot up. Pornography? Now that was something to be concerned about. And how had he even accessed it?

"And every day there were so many taking extra time from breaks and getting back late from lunch. It was appalling. Almost too much to list, but I managed it. Excel is a wonderful program."

"Thank you, Shelia. I will look at everything carefully."

She gave me one swift nod. "I'm only trying to help." She straightened her jacket once more and turned on her very-high-heeled shoes. She froze at the door and turned back. "I hope you had a nice vacation," she said stiffly.

I didn't believe a word of it. After all, I had just taken my office back. "Thank you, Shelia." I almost told her that I hoped she enjoyed being in charge. I didn't. Because I didn't feel that way at all.

"Oh. I straightened things up a bit in here. So it would be more organized. I think you will see it is more efficient."

Now I stiffened. God. What had she done?

Before I could respond, she smiled and walked out of my office.

It took me a little while to see all that she had done. It took me all day to find some of the things I needed and used. For one thing, the postcard with all my passwords that I kept taped to the bottom of my pull-out drawer was gone.

I found it in the folder she left, with a sticky note that reminded me company passwords should never be accessible to the "general population."

It was going to be a long day.

I pulled out my cell phone. Still no text from Cole. I couldn't help but be disappointed. But then, it wasn't totally unexpected. When he was out on the range with guests, coverage was intermittent at best—part of the reason people went to Black Bear Guest Ranch was to get away from technology.

But that kept me from being able to be only a text away from him.

I'd never cared one way or the other about cell phones before, except to be able to get ahold of Crystal at a moment's notice. I'd never cared about texting either.

Funny how much can change in a week.

THAT LAST morning had been wonderful and terrible and wonderful-terrible all at once.

I couldn't help but think every second that passed was one second closer to being without Cole. My heart was like a stone, even though it jumped every time he looked at me with his beautiful, dark almond eyes and smiled at me.

He got me up very early and, ignoring our morning erections, insisted we get dressed, ignoring also my pleas that we make love. We didn't have much longer to make love.

We stopped at the kitchen, where Cole grabbed a couple of warm cinnamon rolls and put them in a brown paper bag. Then we were off to the stables. We saddled Mystic and Madrigal and rode as fast as I dared across a pasture and into the woods. He took me to another of his secret places, a lovely clearing in the middle of the trees where the warm morning sun shone brightly with golden light.

There he spread out a blanket and, without a word, stripped naked. I didn't have to be asked; I did the same. We were both hard and tumbled to the blanket, face to erection, and brought each other to swift orgasms.

That was when he surprised me again.

He wanted to ride naked.

I was nervous as hell, but we did as he asked—of course—and though the saddle was a little rough on my balls, we rode off into the sunlight. It seemed the clearing was a sort of pocket of grass in a second pasture. It was scary and thrilling at the same time to be riding naked and innocent under the clear sky.

But that's what life was like with Cole.

And my heart ached knowing it was almost over.

Were *we* over?

Was this it?

Was this all there was?

How was I going to be able to return to my world? How was I going to leave all this behind? Leave Cole behind.

The night before, he had called me "my love." Did he mean it? Had that just been some kind of expression? Was it just a rush of feelings because of what had happened that magical week? There was no way he could fall in love with me in just one week, could he?

But looking at him as we trotted along, horses nickering and tossing their heads now and again, looking at him astride that horse like some young but ancient god, I knew....

I was in love with him. Truly in love for the first time in my life.

Truly, madly, deeply....

CHARLEEN'S PHOTOCOPYING had to do with her church. It was for fliers. She had used her own paper. And Horrell & Howes had a policy about that. If you brought your own paper and what you were copying was for nonprofit reasons, all was well with the world. She just hadn't filled out the request sheet. I told her to fill it out, mark it for the day before I left, and bring it back to me. I would take care of it. Her gratitude was palpable.

Thomas's pornography?

Classical paintings by the Old Masters for his art history homework. Edouard Manet's *Luncheon on the Grass*, Duchamp's *Nude Descending a Staircase (No. 2)*, Paul Cezanne's *Baigneurs*, *Sleeping Venus* by Giorgione, *The Birth of Venus* by Botticelli, *La Danse* by Henri Matisse, the classic sculptures of *The Dying Gaul* and Lysippos's *Weary Herakles*. Hardly pornography. The only one I could even sort of think might get under her skin was Andy Warhol's *Resting Boy*. Was Shelia the kind of person who would have books like Flaubert's *Madame Bovary* and Miller's *Tropic of Cancer* burned for the same reason?

It was ridiculous, and I had Thomas fill out some fake paperwork as well.

And finally there was Sloan.

He was using the fax machine for medical paperwork for his mother. It turned out she was dying of cancer. Sloan sat impassive before me as he explained. Except for a tremble I don't think I would have seen if I wasn't looking for it, he kept totally in control. I found I felt humiliated. God. To be going through that. How I knew that feeling. No. No, I would never know what that felt like. But I knew death. I could empathize.

I told Sloan to give me any paperwork in the future and I would fax it on my machine. And I assured him I wouldn't look at it.

He stood up and thanked me and then stopped. Finally some emotion on his face. "Are those photographs from your vacation?" he asked and pointed at my corkboard.

"Yes," I said.

"May I look?"

"Sure," I replied, and he came round to my side of the desk.

"These are great pictures. Wow. Look at you on that horse and... gosh, who is *he*?" He pointed at—of course—Cole. "He's *gorgeous*."

"Yes, he is," I said before I even realized it. "Th-that's C-Cole."

We locked eyes when I stuttered. And why the hell did I stutter? It made me mad at myself.

Then I saw the understanding in his eyes and cursed myself once again for a flash of... what was it? Not shame, surely. Embarrassment? That was just as bad.

Cole was the man I loved and....

"God," I said quietly.

The man I loved.

And how could I have been surprised at that? Because it was true. I was in love. My heart swelled and ached at the knowledge.

"Summer romance?" Sloan asked quietly, and this time I refused to deny what had happened to me. Summer romance was right. I had shared loving with another man.

"Yes," I said, and my heart pounded. It was a first. I was telling Sloan I was gay. It was one thing to tell Amy. Another for Crystal to realize it—hell, she had joyfully approved. But Sloan was practically a stranger.

But a gay one.

And that suddenly made me feel very good. I was a part of something very special. An ancient brotherhood.

One I would no longer refute.

"God, those can be a bitch. At least that's what I've heard. I fell in love with a one-night stand."

"Sloan. I can't stop thinking about him."

"Tell me about it," Sloan said. "I have to be *friends* with him. I see him all the damned time."

"Sloan, I can't even see Cole! He's six hours away!" My heart was aching now.

Sloan sighed. He looked at me. "Does he feel the same way?"

"I think so," I said. *He hasn't called.* "He called me—" I blushed. I was so new at this!

"Yes?" Sloan encouraged.

"—my love." I said it so softly I wasn't sure he heard me.

Sloan smiled.

"Well, if someone that cute called me 'my love,' I sure as shit wouldn't let six hours separate me."

My heart started to pound. "No?"

"No fucking way," he said.

My heart took wing.

"Look," he said, eyes alight. "Let's have lunch."

He grinned, and I couldn't help but do the same.

But he hasn't called.

"I probably shouldn't. I've got all kinds of stuff to catch up on."

He shrugged. "You're the boss."

And then I realized he was right. I was the boss, wasn't I?

"Where do you want to go?"

"THERE'S MY bird," I said and pointed upward.

Cole and I were lying on the blanket again and munching on cinnamon rolls.

"It's a turkey vulture," he informed me.

"A what?" I looked at him askance. Vulture? What a letdown. I had imagined something far more elegant. A hawk or falcon or something. And weren't bald eagles supposed to nest in this part of the country?

Cole nodded. "Ugly up close, but so incredibly graceful. It's their wings. It's like they're floating."

"Floating," I said. "Just like that. So free."

"It's so they can look for food. Dead things."

I looked at him again. "Not very romantic, Cole."

"You telling me I'm not romantic?" He looked at me, his eyes so deep, so breathtaking.

And then we made love.

Afterward, holding each other, we heard the camp bell.

"Jesus," he said sitting up. "That's the one-hour warning!"

And fighting back tears, I scrambled to dress. We jumped onto our horses, and they snorted their disapproval at being taken from the fresh wisps of new grass they had found.

Cole helped me pack, and it was all I could do not to cry. When I looked at him, he seemed so crisp, so efficient. All business. If I didn't know better, I would've thought he had affairs with all his guests.

I knew it wasn't true.

Somehow it hurt anyway. I was dying. He looked so… so nonchalant.

But then, just as we were snapping my suitcase closed, he turned to me, and I saw that his eyes were wet. "Neil. Daddy. D-don't…."

When he didn't finish his sentence, I asked him, "Don't what?"

"Don't forget me?"

"My God!" I cried out while another part of me marveled that I had been using His name for days—something I had refused to do for years. "I will never forget you. Never! You set me free."

He shook his head. "No. That was you. I... I...."

"Yes?" I asked, heart dying. Hoping.

We looked at each other for what felt like forever. "N-nothing," he said.

Then he took my suitcase, and we walked to the main hall.

We'd missed breakfast entirely, between riding naked and making love and packing. He took me to the kitchen and was able to get the cook to assemble me a big sandwich made of egg and bacon—those thick Black Bear Guest Ranch slabs. Heart attack between two slices of homemade bread.

Then we joined the others.

And there were a lot of them. Sixty people at least, and that wasn't counting the wranglers.

We got there just in time to hear Darla say, "Good morning, everyone. To everyone who is leaving today, we hope you had a wonderful time." And her eyes found mine in the crowd. "I hope we'll see you again." She looked away. "Vincent and I loved having you, and our staff did too. They tell me you're about the best darned group we've ever had."

"She always says that" came Amy's whispered echo in my ear.

"For all our new guests, welcome! I'm Darla Clark...."

I couldn't listen, and I pulled away from Cole and headed as fast as I could to Amy's car. It was parked in a handicapped space.

"Neil!"

Cole.

I froze and his hand fell on my shoulder. He turned me around.

There were tears in his eyes.

And he kissed me.

It took my breath away.

"You did set me free," he said when we broke away.

"And you" was all I could manage.

Then we were packing the car. Cassie pushed through to give me a hug, and then Leo surprised me by shaking my hand.

"It was nice to meet you," he said. "I'll miss you."

"You will?" I asked and couldn't help but glance at Cole.

He gave me a brave, flickering smile. "You helped Cole. That's all that mattered. And you gave us a story we'll talk about for years. The black bear of Black Bear Ranch!"

Then Vincent and Darla were there, Vincent surprising me by skipping the manly handshake and hugging me roughly instead—"You're a hero," he said—and Darla taking me into her arms, and if she didn't hug me as tight, she hugged me close and long. As we parted she looked up into my eyes and told me not to be a stranger. "*Please,*" she said.

"Really?" I asked.

"Really," she said.

I cleared my throat. "I guess that depends on Cole."

Her eyes grew sharp. "It takes two, Mr. Baxter."

"Neil," I said automatically.

"You come back and I'll call you anything you want."

And then with one long look, I climbed into the car, and when all were aboard, we backed out of the parking spot. But Cole...? He was already gone.

Amy shifted the car into gear and then looked at me.

"You sure?"

I took a breath and almost sobbed. I couldn't answer. I nodded instead.

She shrugged. "Okay."

"What else can I do?" I managed.

"Whatever you want," she replied, and when I didn't answer, she started the car into motion and down the road away from Black Bear Guest Ranch.

"WHAT DID she mean by that?" Sloan asked.

"I don't know. And I wasn't in the frame of mind to ask. Especially with the kids in the backseat."

We were at a local hamburger joint that put McDonald's or Burger King to shame.

"Everyone was inordinately quiet for at least the first half hour we were on the road." And that made it overly uncomfortable as well. Todd kept his face ridiculously close to his electronic game, Robin and Crystal whispered between themselves, and Amy stared at the road. "It was horrible," I said.

"I bet." Sloan nodded sympathetically. "And he hasn't called?"

I shook my head. "We talked last night for a few minutes before he was cut off." It had felt like my heart was being cut out. "He was funny." Warm and distant at the same time.

"Funny?" Sloan asked.

"Like…. Like…. It felt like he didn't want to be on the phone. God, Sloan, I was suddenly reminded of when Crystal—my daughter—had her first kiss when she was a sophomore." This was just a few months before Em died. "I was beside myself, and Emily thought it was so sweet. I wanted to get me a baseball bat with nails sticking out of it, but Em calmed me down." I realized suddenly that Sloan had no idea who "Em" was, but thankfully he wasn't asking. "She said it was normal. But then that was all it took for Crystal to fall in love and fall *hard*. But the boy? He'd lost interest within a day or so and had moved on, and my daughter cried for a week. That really made me want to get that baseball bat, and Em calmed me down about that too. She told me that was normal and that you had to fall in love once and have it end badly. It was a part of it."

My chest grew heavy.

I put my fork down and clenched my hands tightly in my lap. Otherwise I might've started acting like a fool. God! Tears were wanting to come.

"Sloan… is that what this is? *My* 'fall in love and have it end badly'?" Please have it not be so. *Please!* I couldn't stand it.

"I don't know," Sloan said. "I don't know enough. I'm sorry, Neil. I hope not."

He hoped not! Me, it was the worst nightmare I could imagine. I had finally found myself. I was truly happy for the first time in my life. How could I bear getting through this? And after that, what? Go to gay bars and find someone? Look on the Internet? The idea was too horrible to even think about.

"I'm acting like a high school girl, aren't I?" I said.

"Well, I don't know if girls have any exclusivity on what you're feeling, Neil," Sloan said.

And the realization hit and hit hard. "It's just like Amy said…."

Sloan looked at me, waiting for me to continue.

"She said that in a way I am a teenager because I never went through what was natural for me. That what I was going through with

Cole was my inner twenty-something trying to get out. Except it's worse than that. It's my inner fourteen-year-old."

God, I didn't like this. I hated it. How did anyone cope with—

My cell phone made its little *bah-rrrrring* sound. I'd just gotten a text.

I looked at Sloan. He looked at me.

"Well, are you going to look?" he asked.

"It's probably just Crystal."

Sloan sighed. "You won't know if you don't look. Dammit, Neil. The anticipation is killing *me*."

I waited one more heartbeat and then couldn't stand it anymore.

I activated my screen, clicked the message button and…

Missing you more than I can stand—Cole

A joy so immense passed through me, I thought I might faint. I laughed. I *was* a fourteen-year-old!

Me too, I typed back.

There was a long pause while I forgot to breathe.

Bah-rrrrring!

And oh!

I love you was the reply.

The relief was beyond imagining, and I really did think I might cry.

"*Well?*" Sloan asked.

I showed him.

He grinned. And finally he said, "Are you going to type it back?"

I grinned back. Then I did it. I typed it back, heart skipping.

I love you too.

The day went a little better after that.

WE TALKED every night thereafter. Once or twice at lunch. There were a few places he could ride to get good reception, and he didn't want to use the office phone. Especially the night we masturbated together. Who knew phone sex could be so hot?

And we said, "I love you," a lot! Oh, it was heaven.

And hell.

He was so far away.

But as Sloan said, I wasn't going to let a mere six hours keep me from Cole. Not when he felt for me what I felt for him.

We made plans for six weeks from then. That's when his season had a brief calm period and he hadn't been assigned to any guests. I had no idea how I was going to wait that long.

Crystal teased me about it.

Amy loved it.

Then around seven o'clock Friday evening my doorbell rang. I'd already gotten the pizza—pepperoni—so I couldn't imagine who it was. I went to the door, and there stood Cole.

I was stunned. Numb.

Noises amplified.

Boys several houses down playing basketball in their driveway.

Mr. Mulhaney mowing his yard across the street.

An old lady walking her dog.

And then I leapt forward and took Cole by the collar and pulled him to me and kissed him. Hard. And for the first time in my life, I didn't care what anyone thought of me.

CHAPTER 15
An Unexpected Suggestion (Request)

AND SO we started our long-distance relationship—which was both heaven and hell. Heaven when we were together, hell when we were apart.

And boy, the "together" truly was heaven.

A six-hour drive wasn't so bad when you knew who was waiting for you at the end. But it was pretty bad when you were driving home.

It was October, and I was at Black Bear, which had officially closed for the season the week before. Cole was in the corral giving a local riding lessons—just because there were no staying guests didn't mean everything had to stop quite yet. I was planting some bulbs out along the parking lot when Darla came up to me.

"Hey, Neil," she said. "You have a moment to talk?"

From where I was kneeling, I looked up and wiped my sweaty forehead. "Sure."

I got up and dusted off my hands as best as I could, and I followed her to the house. Darla pointed to the porch swing before she went inside and then returned with a pitcher of lemonade.

It was delicious. Freshly made if not locally grown.

She looked at me long and hard.

"Darla?" I asked, growing concerned when she didn't say anything.

"This thing between you and Cole...."

What about it? I wondered. Hadn't she said she supported it?

"I think it's pretty clear that you two are serious."

My chest swelled, and I grinned foolishly. "God, yes." Once again tears pinpricked the corners of my eyes. Very serious. I was *so* in love.

She nodded.

"And I guess Cole is going to come stay with you for a few months? While we're closed for the season?"

Now it was my turn to nod.

"See if you two feel the same way about each other when you are with each other day by day instead of just the occasional weekend?"

Occasional was right. Cole had to be at Black Bear on the weekends. That was the last day and first day of each group of guests. Leaving wasn't a good thing. And while I wasn't sixteen, driving those six-hour trips on Friday after work and driving back on Sunday so I could be at work was taking its toll.

"Yes," I said. And I couldn't wait.

"That's the point where we see," she said. "When you find out your love leaves dirty socks all over the place or they squeeze the toothpaste from the top instead of the bottom or refuse to put on a new roll of toilet paper when they take the last of one before and there you are sitting there with nothing to wipe with."

I blushed. I'd only heard Darla talk like a regular person once or twice. Seeing this part of her was… well… surprising. She was normally the personification of a country lady. Mentioning wiping was somehow beneath her. As if country ladies didn't have such bodily functions that needed caring for.

"The third time I fell in the toilet in the middle of the night was almost Vincent's end. But after he started peeing on the seat during one of his sleepwalking bathroom visits and I had to sit in that too, I knew I had to either kill him or accept that as a part of him and learn to look before I sat."

I laughed. It was that or flee.

"I guess, ma'am."

"Ma'am?" She laughed with me. Then she said, "So I guess you'll find out."

I nodded. Somehow I thought Cole and I would manage.

"And so will he."

I smirked. Cole had already found out that I squeeze the toothpaste from wherever I pick it up. He didn't like it.

"But you know what? Somehow I think you and Cole will manage."

I smiled all the more as she once again seemed to be able to read minds. It was a gift of hers. Good skill for her to have out here in the middle of nowhere.

"I think it's what you said to me," I replied. "About how you believe we come together in life for a reason. I truly do believe Cole and I were brought together. I don't know how or by what or who." God? I wasn't quite there yet, but I knew that's what Cole thought, and I was content to let him do so.

"I was thinking the same thing." Darla nodded and took a sip of her lemonade.

"You know, I believe Cole had me the minute I saw his picture on your website."

Darla cocked her head back and laughed. "Oh! That's wonderful, Neil. I love it."

I smiled.

"You know what else I been thinkin'?" she asked me.

"No," I said. "Tell me."

She winked. "I feel like there's plenty of room for you here at Black Bear."

The words shocked me. "What?"

"Your daughter's going away to college, right?"

I nodded.

"So what say you leave that house and that town where you've been living and all those ghosts. Get away. Make a new home. We'd be glad to have you."

Here? "But…. But what would I do here? I'm no wrangler, although I've finally gotten over being afraid of horses." Wondrous Mystic started that. And then Cole's careful guidance had finished it.

"Maybe not, but I sure can, and I miss it."

"Miss it?" I asked.

"Being a wrangler, son. Riding every day. Leading the trails. Getting on that horse for more than the weekly surprise when I come riding in and shooting those targets."

I nodded.

"And didn't I hear tell about how you're some kind of an office manager? And that you like it?"

"Yeah," I said. "A supervisor. It was a surprise too. How much I like it."

"Mrs. Radcliff—Amy—said you have lots of experience working with the public. She says you can calm down the angriest customers there are."

Yes. But I was glad I only had to take on the angriest. I had been glad to get off the phones. But then, that had been a different time. Only a year, but a lot can change in a year.

"It sure would be nice if you took over the office and gave me more time with the horses."

My mouth fell open.

"Well, Neil! What did you think I was gettin' at?"

"Just like that?" I asked.

"Just like that. I've got a good feeling about you."

"You do?" I felt a sudden flash of fear. "Darla, isn't this taking things a little fast? Cole and I... I mean, we've only been... ah...."

"Seeing each other?" Darla filled in.

I nodded.

"If this living together test works, it sure would be a good solution. Long-distance relationships suck cow patties. Before we were married, when Vincent was in the Navy, when he got stationed overseas? I thought I'd die that long year. Toilet seats or not. I believe you bein' away from that boy is just as much hell for you as it is for him."

I sighed.

"What I think you should do—if you two decide you like living together, and I think you will—what I think you should do is leave that city job of yours. Live here at the Bear with your man."

Live here?

"Would that be a problem? You in love with the big city? Would livin' in the country be too laid back for you?"

Would it be a problem? I suddenly wanted to laugh. The idea filled me with a joy like I had never known that threatened to come out in whatever way it could.

"Really?" I exclaimed.

"Yup. I think this is just the place for you, Neil. And I think Cole's just the man." She looked at me.

I grinned. I couldn't help it. "Do you trust me running your office?" I asked.

"I do or I wouldn't've offered you the job."

"Oh my God, Darla."

"Is that a yes?"

"Is what a yes?" said Cole, stepping up on the porch and looking all kinds of gorgeous.

Without taking my eyes off my love, I answered.

"Yes, Darla. That's a big yes!"

EPILOGUE
Uncle Cole

AMY'S CAR pulled into the parking lot, and before Cole and I could start down the porch steps, Crystal was out the door and running up the walk. "Pop," she yelled and threw her arms around me. She kissed me and hugged me all the tighter.

"Oh, baby," I said, "I've missed you so much."

"Me too, Poppa." She pulled back and then launched herself at Cole. "Hey, Uncle Cole."

"Uncle?" he said.

"Well, you sure aren't my stepmom!"

We all laughed.

"Nope," I agreed, looking at my man—*my man!*—from top to bottom. "Cole is no stepmom."

Oh, the look Cole gave me!

"Hello, stranger" sounded Amy's familiar voice.

I nearly ran down the steps and into her arms. "Oh, Amy, how have you been?"

"I've been good," she said, stepping back. "I have someone I'd like you to meet."

A man joined us, tall, lean, balding, but handsome.

"This is Brice. He's the one who bought your house."

I smiled and shook his hand. "It's nice to meet you, Brice."

"Likewise," he replied. "I've heard a lot about you."

"Uh-oh."

"All of it good, so don't worry." He looked to my left. "And you must be Cole."

"I am," Cole answered and took his hand. "I was surprised to hear Amy was bringing another new guest to Black Bear."

"I've been looking forward to it. I used to love riding horses as a teenager. I can't wait."

"We figure we'll put you up at the cabin down by the creek," Cole said. "It's really nice."

"Wonderful," I added.

Amy cleared her throat. "I don't think that'll be necessary," she said and held out her hand. An engagement ring sparkled brightly in the sunlight.

"Oh my God," I shouted and pulled her into my arms. "When did this happen?"

Amy blushed. "It's been happening. He came to look at your house, bought it, and then decided he wanted me too. I was afraid to say anything, you know? Owen being gone only a year and a half."

"Oh, Amy," I said and kissed her. "You shouldn't have worried."

"I popped the question last week," Brice said.

"We figured we'd wait another year," Amy said. "Then, if it's all right, we'd get married right here."

That got a loud whoop from Cole and set me to laughing.

People did get married at Black Bear Guest Ranch, all right.

"Going to replace some old memories with new ones?" I asked her.

"Not replace," Amy said. "Add to."

Darla and Vincent came out onto the porch.

"Good morning, everyone," Darla said. "To all of you who are leaving today, we hope you had a wonderful time and we hope you'll be back. We loved having you, and the staff says you're about the best darned group we've ever had."

"She always says that," Amy whispered in Brice's ear.

"For all our new guests, I'm Darla Clark, and this is my husband, Vincent. Welcome to Black Bear!"

I reached out and took Cole's hand. When he smiled at me, looked at me with those eyes dancing, I knew there could be no more welcome place on Earth.

I knew something else as well.

I believe we all come together in life for a reason.

And sometimes, this time, that reason was love.

B.G. THOMAS lives in Kansas City with his husband of more than a decade and their fabulous little dog. He is lucky enough to have a lovely daughter as well as many extraordinary friends. He has a great passion for life.

B.G. loves romance, comedies, fantasy, science fiction, and even horror—as far as he is concerned, as long as the stories are character driven and entertaining, it doesn't matter the genre. He has gone to literature conventions his entire adult life where he's been lucky enough to meet many of his favorite writers. He has made up stories since he was a child; it is where he finds his joy.

In the nineties, he wrote for gay magazines but stopped because the editors wanted all sex without plot. "The sex is never as important as the characters," he says. "Who cares what they are doing if we don't care about them?" Excited about the growing male/male romance market, he began writing again. Gay men are what he knows best, after all—since he grew out of being a "practicing" homosexual long ago. He submitted a story and was thrilled when it was accepted in four days. Since then the stories have poured out of him. "It's like I'm somehow making up for a lifetime's worth of stories!"

"Leap, and the net will appear" is his personal philosophy and his message to all. "It is never too late," he states. "Pursue your dreams. They will come true!"

Website/blog: bthomaswriter.wordpress.com

B.G. Thomas
J. Scott Coatsworth
Jamie Fessenden
Michael Murphy

A MORE
PERFECT
UNION

On June 26, 2015, the Supreme Court of the United States made a monumental decision, and marriage equality became the law of the land.

That ruling made history—but what about the gay men who waited and wondered if the day would ever come when they could stand beside the person they love and say "I do"?

Here, four accomplished authors—gay married men—offer their take on that question as they explore same-sex relationships, love, and matrimony. Men who thought legal marriage was a right they would never have. Men who now stand legally joined with the men they love. With this book, they share the magic of dreams that came true—in tales of fantasy and romance with a dose of personal experience in the mix.

To commemorate the anniversary of full marriage equality in the US, this anthology celebrates the idea of marriage itself--and the universal truth of it that applies to us all, gay or straight.

www.dreamspinnerpress.com

Seasons of Love: Book One

Sloan McKenna is going through a tough time. His beloved mother has recently passed away, leaving him her house and beautiful garden. But should he keep the house? Sell it? To make matters worse, he's in love with one of his best friends, Asher, a man who can't (or won't) love him back.

Sloan's neighbor, Max Turner, is married to an ambitious woman with far-reaching dreams, including moving the family to France. But Max is happy teaching at the local college and living in their nice, quiet town. Then he discovers his fourteen-year-old son is not only gay, but out and proud as well. That throws him into complete disarray, for more than one reason....

When Max's wife leaves on a two-month business trip to Paris, circumstances throw the two men together. As they become friends, Sloan finds himself falling in love with Max, who is completely unavailable... just like Asher. As for Max, he is discovering that both his son's coming out and his new friendship with Sloan are stirring up feelings he thought buried long ago. Spring is a time for rebirth—Is there any way the two men can find happiness and a new beginning?

www.dreamspinnerpress.com

Seasons of Love: Book Two

Scott Aberdeen doesn't believe in Santa Claus, the Easter Bunny, or God. Or love—at least, he knows no one will ever love him. After all, he has carried a torch for his best friend Sloan for a decade, hoping his feelings will be returned one day. But when Sloan finds springtime love with another man, Scott's fantasies are crushed and his skepticism confirmed.

Cedar Carrington, raised by rock star parents, leads a free-spirited, nomadic life, never staying in one place for long. Due to a dark past he refuses to share or even think about, he is willing to let men into his bed for sex, but never for the night.

When Scott finds himself camping in the middle of nowhere with over a hundred men who all believe in love—and faeries and a magickal gay brotherhood—he's pretty sure he's in the wrong place. And when Cedar connects with cynical, critical Scott, he wonders how he could be falling in for this man of all men. But hearts and lives have been transformed at the Heartland Men's Festival before, and it might be just the place where two very different men can release their pain and find true love at last.

www.dreamspinnerpress.com

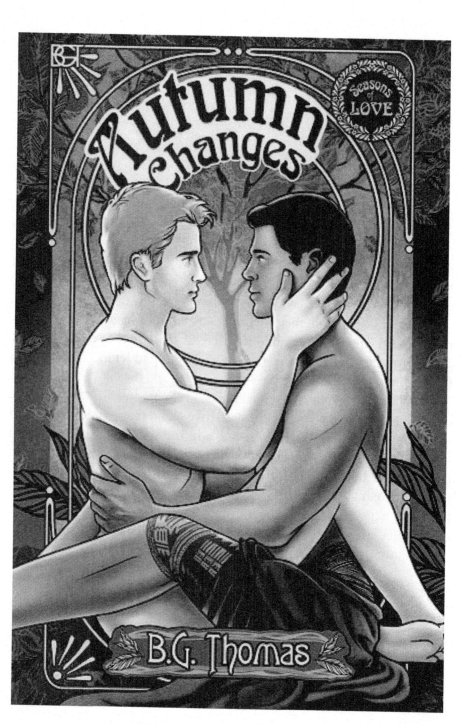

Seasons of Love: Book Three

Asher Eisenberg is a brilliant actor, destined for fame and fortune. But a traumatic incident in his past has caused him to reject his Jewish heritage and hide from everyone behind walls of arrogance and selfishness, and he blurs his loneliness with a lot of sex and alcohol. When he meets Peniamina Faamausili, however, he strangely can't stop thinking about the young man.

Peni is struggling with his sexuality, the Mormonism he was raised in, and the Samoan heritage that calls to him. He longs to receive the pe'a—the traditional Samoan tattoos-- and learn more of his people's ways. He has no interest in a man like Asher, who appears to use men and put them aside and whose drinking can't help but remind him of the drunk driver who killed his father. But he can't deny his attraction to Asher and finally agrees to a date if Asher can go thirty days without a drink.

Asher is about to go on a journey that will awaken him to his friends, his past, his future, and even to love. But that awakening could well demand the sacrifice of the dream he holds most dear.

www.dreamspinnerpress.com

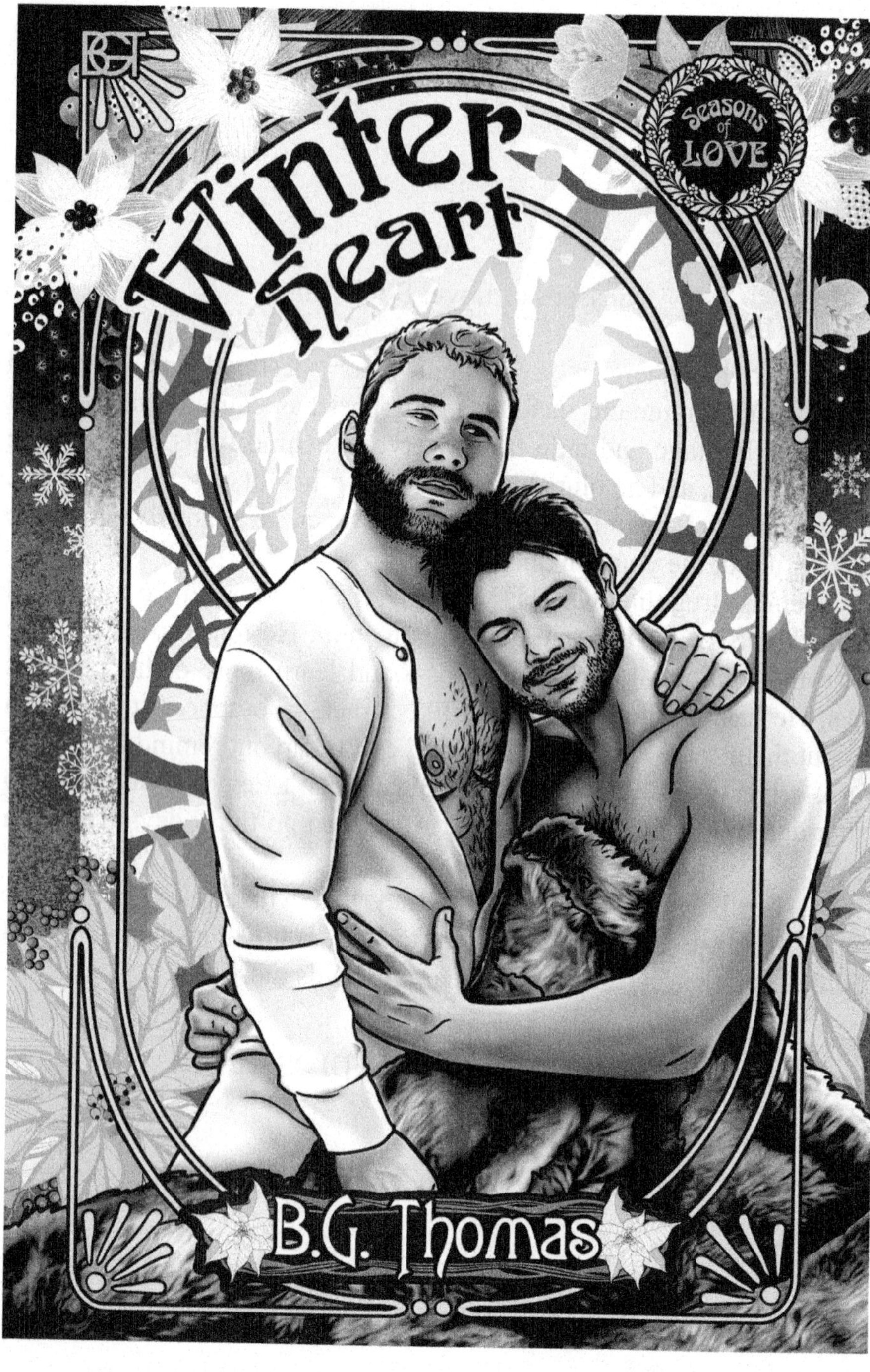
Winter Heart
Seasons of LOVE
B.G. Thomas

Seasons of Love: Book Four

For over ten years, Wyatt Dolan defined himself as the lover of Howard Wallace. Howard made sure Wyatt's self-worth depended on that role. So when Howard dumps him, he is lost at sea in a storm without a rudder. If it wasn't for his supportive friends, he doesn't know what he'd do. Finally, after a series of disasters, he escapes to Camp Sanctuary—a sacred place to him—where he can be alone, try to put his past behind him, and find a new direction for his life.

Kevin Owens is a lonely man. He is very intelligent—several apps he created have gone on to make him a comfortable living—but he is also quite shy and is uncomfortable making conversation. The death of his dear friend and former lover after a long illness leaves him grieving, confused, and adrift. Then a dream guides him to Camp Sanctuary, only to find that the one cabin with a wood-burning stove has already been reserved. And worse, by a man he's had a secret crush on for years—Wyatt Dolan.

When a snowstorm knocks out power at the Camp, Wyatt and Kevin must share the same cabin to stay warm, and very soon, magickal things begin to happen.

www.dreamspinnerpress.com

FOR **MORE** OF THE **BEST GAY ROMANCE**

CPSIA information can be obtained
at www.ICGtesting.com
Printed in the USA
BVOW06s0236080118
504328BV00004B/152/P